CINNAMON AND THE CLOVE CONSPIRACY

THE CATMINT CHRONICLES BOOK 3

AMANDA STERCZYK

CONTENTS

1

Rowan Thorne

Monday
Five Days Before the Great Harvest Bake Off

I had just finished tidying up the kitchen when I heard the bell above the shop door chime. The last time I had rushed out and left a mess behind, it hadn't been pretty. Both the chaos in the kitchen and the aftermath when Cinnamon, my sometimes-talking cat, had accidentally ingested the remnants of Sleep Salve that had littered the floor. I was adamant with myself that I wouldn't leave a mess and that I wouldn't be late for my appointment with the Blooms.

Cursing myself for not locking up, I sighed as I left the kitchen. It was husband-wife business owners, Mortimer and Hortense Slack. I was used to seeing Mortimer earlier in the day, for his noon-time coffee, but he usually came alone.

"Hello Mortimer! Hello Hortense! What brings you to Black Thumb Betty's? I was just about to close for the day."

Mortimer could talk your ear off, and I didn't feel like trying to drop subtle clues with him today. Nor did I want Hortense, widely considered the village gossip, to know where I was headed. I wanted to finish up with them and get going.

I had had few truly quiet days since inheriting Black Thumb Betty's Café & Herb Shop from my long-lost, now-deceased Aunt Betty. My father's impending arrival next month was weighing on my mind in these hectic times. How could I show him I was responsible enough to run my own business if I wasn't even organized?

The lack of down time had negatively impacted my training. There was still so much to learn, not just about running my own business in a new country, but also my aunt's special formulations that drove her "after hours" business. This included the blend I had been working on today.

After several failed attempts to recreate Betty's Recollection Restorative, I was trying a new blend. Goodbye catmint, hello ground cloves. Now I just needed to move this conversation with Mortimer and Hortense along so I could get the new formulation to my test subject.

Mortimer was as large as Hortense was tiny, but she definitely wore the pants in their union. Hortense was standing with her arms crossed, a stern look on her face. Since moving to England last month, I had known the owners of the village kitchen goods shop, the Copper Kettle, to be generally friendly people—gossip about who had burned what at the last bake sale aside.

Judging from Hortense's current demeanor, I was certain this wasn't a social call. Nor did they seem interested in purchasing a hot beverage. Mortimer looked more uncomfortable than confrontational, and I suspected Hortense had dragged him along for moral support. Or to be her mouthpiece. He looked to me like he wanted the ground to open up below him and swallow him whole. Hortense nudged him in the ribs, compelling him to get the ball rolling. Mouthpiece it was.

"Well, ahem, yes, you see, Rowan," he was off to a blundering start, and Hortense made her dismay known to both of us.

"Oh, just spit it out, Mortie."

"Yes, yes, quite right, Hortense."

"Spit what out?" I felt like I needed to speed things up if I had any chance of not being late.

"Well, you see, Hortense has heard..."

Oh no, it was shaping up to be a gossip-fueled accusation, of that I was certain.

Mortimer finally found some courage and sputtered out the reason for their non-social call. "Well, she's heard that Pennyworth's Provisions has run out of ground cloves."

"Oh? I'm confused. Why are *you* telling me about cloves. I thought the Copper Kettle only sold kitchen goods and cookware. Why would you be concerned about the supply of cloves at Pennyworth's?"

I felt badly that my question was making Mortimer uncomfortable when it was clearly Hortense who was pulling the strings here. But I knew if I let her see me crumble, I would be the next source of her gossip. And that could hurt business at Black Thumb Betty's—the shop I had only just saved from closure. I also found it hard to believe that I had bought up Pennyworth's entire stock of cloves. Sure, I had bought *a lot*, but the shelf wasn't completely empty when I left with my purchases. Leave it to Hortense to blow things out of proportion.

"Quite right, Rowan. You see, Hortense is fiercely protective of fall baking spices. She's a judge at The Great Harvest Bake Off and she wants to ensure all contestants have what they need for a fair competition."

This wasn't making any sense to me. Was Hortense actually accusing me of hoarding cloves? Was this some kind of clove conspiracy? I wanted to challenge her on it, but I knew I was going to be late if they stayed much longer. It was time to eat some humble pie and mend fences later.

"Gosh, that makes total sense to me. I'm sorry if my large purchase of ground cloves put any bakers' recipes at risk. I'd be happy to share what's left of my stash. I've been tweaking some of my beverage recipes, and I needed a fair amount of cloves to experiment with just the right blend."

Crossing my fingers behind my back, I hoped they wouldn't ask for more details. My comments were only partially false. Most of the cloves were for beverages, but not for paying customers. I had decided that cloves would be a suitable substitute for catmint in my experiments with helping Cinnamon talk, the Reverend sleep, and Elspeth recover her memory. Thankfully, Mortimer seemed satisfied with my answer. He put his arm around Hortense's shoulders, turning to her as he spoke.

"See, Hortie, no conspiracy here. Just a love of cloves."

How odd that he called it conspiracy, when I had just been thinking it might have been a conspiracy on their part. Yet another way the village of Cresswell-on-Wyrd was throwing up coincidences and connections. I was nodding along with Mortimer's comments, gently trying to corral them out the door.

"Very true. I do love the warmth that cloves bring to herbal blends, especially during this late fall weather. Again, if any bakers are in need before Mrs. Pennyworth is able to restock, please do send them my way."

Hortense started to sputter in an attempt to challenge me further, but Mortimer was having none of it. He turned her gently towards the door that I was now holding open for them. As they exited the shop, he turned towards me.

"Sorry to disturb, Rowan. I hope you won't hold it against us and will still frequent the Copper Kettle."

"You know it! I'll be there next time I'm in need of kitchen supplies. Bye!"

Locking the door, I leaned against it and heaved a sigh of relief. Then I hightailed it back to the kitchen, grabbing my supplies in a whirlwind of activity. Time to hit the road.

2

I was running late. Again. My internal clock still hadn't adjusted to my new life in the quirky British village of Cresswell-on-Wyrd, or COW as I liked to call it. But it wasn't entirely my fault. If Mortimer and Hortense hadn't showed up when they did, I wouldn't be rushing this time. Or at least, not as much.

I still found it difficult to believe I'd only been in this village less than a month, and so much had happened. The crisp fall weather had been a welcome surprise, it was so similar to the weather back in New York City at this time of year. For me, fall felt like renewal and time to set new goals, start new projects. Little did I know this fall was going to be the biggest new project of them all.

As I turned to lock the door, I thought about how much had changed in the past month. Not only had I discovered I had a long-lost aunt—Betty of the Black Thumb Betty's—I also learned she had died and left me her shop. A shop that required me to keep regular hours and be available for customers. And, of course, there was Cinnamon, the sometimes-talking cat.

All these individuals relying on me was the reason I was running late. In my past life as a fully remote data analyst in New York City, I had kept my own hours, with no one expecting anything else from me. Now, though, I had responsibilities and commitments...not to mention friends.

A quick glance at my watch told me I would be at least 10 minutes late. I had promised Piper Bloom that I would close up early and head to Blooming Brews, the tea shop that she ran with her identical twin sister, Petunia. I had experimented with a new formulation to try with her mother, Elspeth. We were hoping this new blend of Betty's herbal-based remedy would slow down Elspeth's rapidly progressing dementia, and also potentially reverse it.

Piper Bloom was anxiously awaiting my arrival inside Blooming Brews. Although we ran competing tea shops in the village, there was no competition between us. In fact, we had been working together to help her mother recover her memory. Sadly, it was being wiped away quite quickly by dementia. Piper and her twin sister, Petunia, needed my help to fine-tune my Aunt Betty's herbal remedy called Recollection Restorative. Hopefully, without the side effects we had discovered recently—visions of Cinnamon singing and dancing had been chalked up to too much catmint in the blend.

As I thought of Elspeth, I caught a glimpse of her up ahead. The sound of crackling leaves under her feet seemed to disorient her momentarily. She had just turned out from Lover's Lane onto Sycamore Row. But instead of turning towards me, she was heading away from the village center. Knowing the twins always accompanied her on walks, I picked up my pace to catch up with her.

"Elspeth, Elspeth! Wait for me." Although she seemed to pause when she heard me call out her name, her pace picked up too. In her confused state, her behavior could be unpredictable, and I didn't want her to wander into the road. I caught up with her just as she neared the busier-than-usual roundabout at the edge of the village. Grabbing her elbow, I gently steered her away from the road.

"Do I know you?" The look of confusion on her face was not uncommon, she rarely remembered anyone these days, including her own daughters. I smiled warmly and nodded my head.

"You do. I'm Rowan, Betty Thorne's niece."

Although Betty was deceased, she and Elspeth had collaborated on herbal remedies when Betty first moved to COW many years ago. A flicker of recognition appeared in Elspeth's eyes and she relaxed immediately. Long-ago memories and people still held some real estate in her brain, and my mention of Betty had convinced her to trust me. She allowed me to continue guiding her towards Lover's Lane and the Bloom family tea shop.

Desperate cries of "Mum!" could be heard in the distance. It sounded like Piper and Petunia had split up to search for their confused and wandering mother. Coming towards us was Piper, who tilted her head to the side as she processed her mother walking along with me. That head tilt seemed oddly familiar to me, but I couldn't immediately place it.

Piper placed her thumb and index finger in her mouth, turned around, and whistled loudly. I could see Petunia further down Sycamore Row, running at full speed from Smuggler's Lane. When Petunia caught up to Piper, they hugged before heading towards us. Their relief was palpable.

As they walked towards me, I smiled at their identicalness. The only clue as to who was who was the length of their flowing auburn hair, with Petunia's being one inch shorter than Piper's. They even shared the same smattering of freckles across their noses.

I smiled and waved, while Elspeth's reaction to seeing her daughters approaching was one of non-recognition. She seemed to be having one of her bad days. The twins picked up speed and ran towards us, talking over each other to thank me for finding their mother. As they hugged her, she still showed no signs of recognizing her own flesh and blood. I chimed in to let them know Elspeth hadn't been frightened by my presence.

"I reassured your mother by reminding her that Betty is my aunt. Otherwise, I'm not sure she would have accompanied me."

"Oh Mum, we were so worried about you." Piper spoke first, though Petunia was chomping at the bit to have her say too.

"We can't have you wandering on your own, Mum, it's just too dangerous."

I decided to keep it to myself that Elspeth had been on the verge of wandering into traffic. Piper and Petunia were already overwhelmed with caring for their mother, and no harm had come to her. I didn't want to add to their stress level.

"It's a good thing I was running late. I saw her as I ran out of the shop."

Petunia took Elspeth by the arm and continued walking towards Blooming Brews. Piper pulled me back slightly, wanting to speak with me privately. I turned to face her, holding up my basket that contained the latest formulation of Recollection Restorative.

"Less catmint this time, so hopefully the strange visions won't come back."

"Yes, and hopefully Mum remembers us and not just long-forgotten memories of Betty. No offense, Rowan."

"None taken. I totally get where you're coming from. We'll get this sorted, you have my word."

Thinking about my last statement, Piper stared off into the distance. I had seen my father do the same thing many times in my life. At that moment, Piper seemed a lot like dear Reginald Thorne. Shaking my head to clear that odd thought, I wondered if perhaps it was just a British mannerism.

I patted Piper on the arm and pointed towards the village shops. She nodded and continued walking, no longer staring off in the distance but still circumspect.

"What are you thinking about?"

"This morning, a social worker from the County Health Authority visited us. It seems they've received reports of Mum's wandering. I'm afraid Petunia has been distracted lately when she is with her."

I had met Petunia first, when she worked as Arthur Nudge's assistant in his London law firm, Nettle & Nudge, who had handled my late aunt's estate. At the time, she had been distracted as well, but mostly because she was so far away from the village and her family.

"What's going on with your sister? I thought she was relieved to return to the village and help you with your mother and the shop."

Piper stopped walking to reflect on my comment. "She was, at first. But I think she's feeling a bit like a third wheel."

"How so?"

Piper threw her hands up in frustration, clearly struggling with this conversation. Reaching out, I patted her arm. "It's okay. If you don't want to talk about it, we don't have to."

She shook her head, smiling wanly. "No, no, it helps to

get it off my chest. I just didn't realize how much it was bothering me."

"Which part?"

"Well, all of it, really. I know Petunia's doing her best. But I got so used to managing the shop and Mum on my own, I sort of developed a routine that worked. Petunia feels lost with the new shop set-up, and having her back in the mix has caused our Mum to be even more confused than before."

I squeezed Piper's arm and gently motioned towards the shop again. Nodding, Piper continued walking, albeit more slowly. There was more she wanted to share with me. My silence allowed her to continue.

"More than once lately, Petunia has had my Mum on a walk through the village when she got distracted."

"Distracted by what?" I prodded, trying to keep my words to a minimum.

"By children. When she sees them, she gets all excited and watches them like a hawk. She would love to be a nanny or au pair. But there are currently no open positions in the vicinity."

I filled in the blanks. "And she doesn't want to leave the village, because she feels like she'd be abandoning you and your mother again."

Piper seemed relieved that I was understanding her predicament and not judging their family.

"You both have a lot on your plates. How does all this relate to this morning's social worker visit?"

"Petunia knows that being out in public with Mum requires extreme vigilance. She's prone to wandering off unaccompanied and getting lost. It's been happening more frequently when the two of them are together."

"Everyone in the village knows about your mother. And they all look out for her. So why did they visit today?"

"Well, they're concerned for her safety. They told us if we can't keep her from wandering, they'll commit her to an assisted care facility."

Piper choked up as she spoke. The toll of losing her mother to a locked medical facility was written all over her face. Putting my basket on the ground, I grabbed Piper in a hug. My previous aversion to public displays of affection disappeared when I was near one of the twins. There was a connection between us that made me want to comfort them when needed, even though they were older than me.

"We'll get this sorted, Piper. Please try not to worry."

Hiccoughing as she pulled away, Piper picked up my basket and tipped her head towards the lane. My steps matched her pace, and we caught up with Petunia and Elspeth in no time. Her unspoken acknowledgement of my support seemed to have lightened the invisible weight she had been carrying on her shoulders.

Although still confused, Elspeth also appeared less anxious than even a few minutes earlier. Petunia, on the other hand, had stress written all over her face. I wanted to do everything I could to help Piper and Petunia hang on to their mother. Not to mention keeping the family together and happy in the village.

3

My walk back to my own shop happened after dark. I hadn't realized how long we had been watching Elspeth after she consumed quite a lot of the Recollection Restorative tea. When she fell asleep in the back room of Blooming Brews, I sat with Piper and Petunia for a spell. Elspeth didn't wake with strange visions of a singing, dancing Cinnamon, so we were cautiously optimistic that this latest version would work. Having swapped out the catmint for a small amount of ground cloves, I hoped I had interpreted Betty's cryptic notes correctly.

As I approached Black Thumb Betty's, I could see a pile of mail on the mat. Sighing, I shook my head in disappointment. The village mail carrier, Stan Pigeon, was deathly afraid of cats. He refused to push the mail through the slot, fearful that Cinnamon would attack his hand. I reached down and picked up the correspondence before unlocking the shop door. Hungry as I was, I decided to grab a snack before turning in for the night.

Except for bills, there were only two envelopes of interest to me. Both were addressed to me, with no return address. And no paid postage on the envelopes either. Sitting down at the kitchen table, I tossed everything but one envelope down. After ripping it open, I could smell smoke. It was subtle, but it was there nonetheless. The page I pulled out was burnt along the bottom, erasing some of the words. Squinting, I could just make out my Aunt Betty's signature, similar to versions I had seen on old paperwork lying around the shop. Where the heck had this little gem been? My aunt had been dead for more than two months. Was this a message from beyond the grave? Another mystery that needed solving, I surmised.

I continued scanning the page for clues. Further up was one of her famous sayings, this one new to me:

To remember what I knew, you must trust the spice that opens the tongue.

Leaning forward over the page, I furrowed my brow. What could this possibly mean? Which spice would open the tongue?

This was definitely something I'd need to discuss with Tilda, my part-time employee and partner in tea experimentation. I hadn't seen her much in the past few days. Since she had moved to Arthur Nudge's home on the edge of the village, her forays to the shop were less frequent.

Having vacated her suite above Wyrd Remedies & Chemist over a falling out with new chemist and landlord, Gideon Place, Tilda was avoiding Sycamore Row and a potential run-in with Gideon. He was still bitter over her departure and blamed Tilda when the Village Council banned short-term rentals in Cresswell-on-Wyrd. But it was his own doing, after he admitted at the last council meeting that he had entered Tilda's suite without permission and stolen documents that didn't belong to him.

Some villagers had wanted him banished, but cooler heads had prevailed. It was difficult to find qualified pharmacists who were interested in running a shop in a village of this size. Gideon had received a fine, a letter was filed with the meeting minutes, and a subsequent impromptu vote to ban short-term rentals was the nail in the coffin. Not really a bad punishment, all things considered.

Confused by both its appearance and message, I placed the burnt paper on the table. Why would someone want to burn a page written by Betty? And why return it to me now? I had more questions than answers at this point.

Next, I reached for the second unstamped envelope. Inside this one was another single sheet of paper, not burned like the last one. Six simple words were scratched across the middle of the page:

Leave now.
You're not wanted here.

It was ominous and somewhat threatening. Not to mention anonymous. Who wanted me gone? Was this another threat to Black Thumb Betty's or me directly? This note made me feel less safe, and I pulled the edges of my cardigan closer together. A knock at the shop door added to my feeling of unease. Rising from the table, I crept towards the swinging doors that separated the kitchen from the customer area in the shop. I slowly pushed the door open and peeked around it. That darned note was making me paranoid too, I realized.

Relief washed over me when I saw that Rory Nudge was standing at the shop entrance, peeking in for signs of life.

Hurriedly, I rushed forward and unlocked the door. Smiling up at the tall, lanky driver for his cousin Arthur's London law firm, I ushered him inside. The smile on his face told me all I needed to know about his unrequited feelings for me. Ever the gentleman, Rory smiled and nodded a greeting. He knew I wasn't ready for a romantic relationship, after leaving my cheating boyfriend behind when I departed New York City for Cresswell-on-Wyrd.

"Rory! It's awfully late. What are you doing in the village? I thought you'd be in London, or at least at your parents' sheep farm. Don't farmers wake up before the sun?"

I ushered him towards the alcove in the front window, my favorite place to sit whether alone or with company. He obliged me by choosing the comfy chair, allowing me to spread out on the facing couch. Rory chuckled as he sat down.

"Yes, I'm surprised I'm here too. It seems Arthur has taken a shine to Tilda being under his roof. We haven't been back to London since last week."

"Well, that certainly is interesting, but not surprising. I feel like love is in the air between those two silver-haired foxes."

"You may be right on that front. And Mum's happy that I've been able to help out with the sheep shearing, not to mention helping Dad with the books. But she's pushing me more to give my notice to Arthur and move back permanently."

"So she's not letting up then?"

Rory shook his sadly. "Not in the least. Earlier this evening, Arthur mentioned he wanted to head into London early tomorrow morning. I will be getting up before the sun, but not because of the farm."

"Maybe this budding romance between Arthur and Tilda will have a net benefit for you."

"How so?"

"Well, if Arthur wants to spend more time with Tilda, maybe he'll retire and move back to the area full-time."

Sitting cross-legged on the couch, I slid my hand under my leg, crossing my fingers when they were out of sight. Rory had no idea that Arthur was indeed mulling over his retirement. It was yet another secret I was being asked to keep, a complex task that was causing me indigestion and awkward moments when my face flushed red. This was one of those times, unfortunately. I was hoping that the dimmed lights in the shop would hide my face color from Rory.

"He might, but I don't want to force his hand if he's not ready. Please keep this information to yourself. It's not the right time to approach him."

"What is it with this village and secrets?" I was exasperated, and my tone did nothing to belie my feelings. Immediately, I regretted my outburst. Rory was gazing at me with the most confused look on his face, causing me to flush red even more.

"Secrets? As in, more than one?"

Darn it, I hoped I hadn't let the cat out of the bag. There was Rory's secret, Arthur's secret, the two anonymous letters I had just received, and the whole talking cat secret.

I waved my hands in the air for effect, hoping it would draw his eyes away from my reddened face. "Let's just say I'm feeling the weight of what's *not* being said and leave it at that."

Rory shrugged in bewilderment and turned to look out the front window. Although dark out, we could both see clouds rolling in to cover up the almost-full moon. He stood to leave, turning on his charming smile.

"So, no movement on the date front, then?"

I laughed as I stood to join him near the door.

"Please. It hasn't even been a month. And that month has been nonstop. I'm not ready to even think about dating. But I promise you'll be the first to know when it's time."

He accepted my answer grudgingly. With a quick wave, Rory dashed out the door. I decided to turn in for the night. The anonymous letters could wait until the morning.

4

Tuesday
Four Days Before the Great Harvest Bake Off

I hadn't seen hide nor hair of Cinnamon before heading to bed the previous night. But he certainly made his presence known this morning. I woke up when I felt a pressure on my chest and a tap on my nose. Opening my eyes, I saw Cinnamon sitting on me, preparing to take another swipe at my face. Groaning, I reached over and grabbed my watch off the bedside table.

"Four fifteen! It's four fifteen, Cinnamon. That is too early for me."

In an attempt to fall back asleep, I rolled over, knocking the cat off my chest. He then took up residence next to my head, meowing incessantly. When I shifted position again, rolling onto my back, Cinnamon climbed back on my chest. In a huff, he turned around until his back side was mere inches from my face. A deep breath told me all I needed to know; I wasn't going back to sleep if Cinnamon had anything to do with it.

"*Fine*. You win. I'm getting up."

That was all the encouragement he needed to jump off my chest and head to the internal not-so-secret staircase that connected my suite with the shop downstairs. Although, it had been a secret when I first arrived in the village. My first evening, I had locked up the shop and walked to the external staircase. It was only the next day when I finally met Tilda, and she had shown me how to shift the bookcase away to access my suite without needing to brave the elements.

This morning, Cinnamon beat me down the stairs. I descended the creaky wooden stairs, making sure to skip the fifth step. It always groaned at the pressure, and I wasn't ready for unwanted noises before my coffee. When I reached the bottom, Cinnamon was standing by the front door. His walking harness sat at his feet, one paw touching the pile. Cinnamon must have raced over to retrieve it from behind the counter.

"A walk? You want to go for a walk at this ungodly hour?"

He continued to paw the leash, almost nodding his head in acknowledgement. Wandering to the counter, I reached over and retrieved one of the many jars of cardamom pods that I had stashed around the shop and my suite. Upon discovering that smelling, rubbing against, or best yet, consuming cardamom, allowed Cinnamon to communicate with humans, I had ordered extra jars and extra cardamom. I even had a baggy of pods in several jacket pockets, lest I be in need of explanation from him when we were on a walk. Although, the cardamom's effects had been waning, and I had yet to discover a suitable alternative to keep the pesky pet talking to me.

"I still don't understand why you feel the need to use a leash. Most cats just wander untethered to their humans."

Cinnamon walked towards me, annoyed that I was expecting a response from him before he had sniffed the crushed cardamom pieces that were now resting in my open palm.

"If you must know," oh boy, I thought, he had woken up on the wrong side of the bed, "I prefer the leash for safety reasons. It brought me comfort, knowing that Betty was at the other end of the leash. She had a habit of wandering off, deep in thought. More than once, I lost her and had to wait outside the shop, in the cold and rain."

His last few words were interspersed with meows and hisses. As I had feared, cardamom's ability to induce Cinnamon's speech was waning. I would need to consult Tilda about introducing different herbs and spices into the mix. She was still teaching me the cryptic code Betty had created to keep her prized recipe book, *Betty's Steep Secrets*, from being read by the casual observer.

I made a mental note to call Tilda later in the morning—at a much more civilized hour—and invite her to the shop to continue our experiments. Leaning down, I gently coaxed Cinnamon into a standing position and attached his harness.

"Are you walking along Sycamore Row to the Community Hall? Or do I have to carry you? I doubt we'll see anyone else along the way."

"I'll walk, since you seem to be so resistant to carrying me. But only because it's early enough to avoid detection."

He was, of course, referring to the village decree that barred pets from walking along Sycamore Row. If you were unlucky enough to be reported, you risked your four-legged companion being carted off to The Royal Society for the

Prevention of Cruelty to Animals (RSPCA) in the next village, Whiskerleigh. Even when Cinnamon annoyed me, like this very early morning, I didn't want to lose him.

"Passive aggressive feline, I see. *Great.*"

Cinnamon was being, well...cat. I realized then that it was going to be a long day. Before I even got a chance to open the door, a loud scraping sound startled us both. What the heck? Who else would be up at this hour and where had the sound originated? Cinnamon bolted towards the back of the shop, in the direction of the now-sealed staircase that led to a secret tunnel. Housing a long-forgotten priest hole, the tunnel ran under Sycamore Row and opened up in a stand of bushes behind Wyrd Remedies and Chemist. Was it possible someone was trying to gain access to Black Thumb Betty's again?

I leaned against the bookcase that hid the entrance, pushing my ear close to the wall. The sound had stopped as quickly as it had started, and Cinnamon had lost interest in investigating it. He pulled me out of my thoughts when he nudged my leg.

"Let's go."

A cat of few words but many aggressive cat sounds this morning, Cinnamon walked back to the front of the shop and stood beside the door. He was waiting for me, but not very patiently. It was going to be a long day indeed. As we meandered quietly along Sycamore Row, my thoughts returned to the sound in the tunnel. Could it be related to the mysterious notes I had just received? I would have to build up the courage to explore the tunnel again but now was not the time. I needed to leave Cinnamon back at the shop and come equipped with a flashlight, maybe even a hammer if the tunnel occupant meant me harm. The notion made me shudder, catching Cinnamon's attention. He looked at me questioningly, but I didn't respond.

"Cat got your tongue? Oh no, that's me, and no, I don't."

He laughed at his own, terrible joke, making up for my silence. I was still imagining who—or what—could possibly have made the noise in the tunnel. Whether or not it was related to the notes, I knew I had to start a suspect list. If only to ease my worried mind and allow me to focus on other matters. Like checking in with Piper about the latest formulation of Recollection Restorative. And getting Tilda to help me with new speech-inducing formulations for Cinnamon. Plus, there was the ever-present need to get the shop organized before my father's visit next month. Yes, the day would be both long and busy. I mused about whether Hortense Slack's name should be added to my list. That was a question I would ponder further when I wasn't so tired.

Hoping to rest my weary eyes for even an hour before my morning opening routine would begin, I gently tugged on Cinnamon's lead. He did not take kindly to it, as he was happily munching on a cobweb along the garden path. Sensing his reticence at wrapping up our early-morning walk, I sighed and picked him up.

"Time to get back to the stable, my young steed."

Cinnamon hissed but didn't respond. Yes, the cardamom had worn off and he couldn't speak. Well, at least in a manner where I could understand him. Given his demeanor and the early hour, I didn't mind at all. We were heading back to Black Thumb Betty's and, with any luck, another hour in bed.

5

It was still too early to get up, I thought to myself. And yet, I'd more or less been tossing and turning for the last hour. I lifted my head and glanced towards the end of the bed. There was Cinnamon, oblivious to my sleepless state. No, he was sawing logs and dreaming of...what? Something, that was for certain. Envy gripped me as I watched him sleep. If only I could fall asleep so easily. Typical cat that he was, Cinnamon could sleep anywhere, anytime. Typical anxiety-fueled young adult that I was, I struggled to both fall and stay asleep.

Finally, I gave up trying and rose for the second time that morning. It was too early to start my shop-opening routine, and I had other plans anyways. My brain was still dwelling on the sounds I had heard in the secret tunnel. Cinnamon had heard them too, so I knew I wasn't imagining it. Now that the entrance in the shop was sealed off permanently, I would have to make my way to the garden path and enter from that direction.

I decided to head down to the shop, first, in case more sounds were emanating from the tunnel. After retrieving the flashlight from behind the counter, I tiptoed towards the old tunnel entrance. Standing there in total silence, I determined that whoever or whatever had made the sounds before was either sleeping or long gone. There was no way to know unless I went down there myself.

After locking up the shop for the second time before the sun had even risen, I turned right and sprinted towards the Community Hall. The path alongside that building would take me directly to the garden path. My nervous energy was the only reason I chose to sprint towards the tunnel entrance. I figured it would keep me from losing my nerve if I got there faster and out of breath.

As I made my way along the garden path, I marveled at the songbirds who had begun their morning routines. It was such a lovely sound, one I had been deprived of when living in the concrete jungle that was New York City. Although I was still adjusting to village life, this was one aspect of the quieter surroundings that I truly appreciated.

The clouds from the night before had blown off and the almost-full moon was lighting the garden path. I would save the flashlight for the darker confines of the secret tunnel. The group of shrubs behind Gideon's shop hid the entrance to the tunnel. I looped around them and was immediately taken off guard. Someone had been there recently. The ground was covered in a few empty food wrappers and a half-full water bottle. Judging from the label, it was a high-end reusable bottle. It looked like the supplies a rambler might carry with them on a walk in the British countryside.

On my first day in Cresswell-on-Wyrd, Arthur had indicated to me that members of the National Rambling Association volunteered to maintain walking paths, including this one. I could see an animal dragging the food wrappers here to lick out the last remnants of food in relative seclusion, but the pricey water bottle was a different story.

Brushing aside the fallen branches that hid the tunnel entrance, I noticed some footprints in the dirt. They looked quite fresh to my untrained eye. Maybe I was making a mountain out of a molehill, and there was no danger lurking below. And yet, my heart rate had picked up speed, not just from the sprint here either.

I reached down to grab the rusty brass ring that opened the trap door. Swinging the door to the side, I jumped back and shone the flashlight down the steps. So far, so good. There were no eyes peering up at me and no one rushed me. I took several deep breaths before I felt confident enough to descend the stairs. Holding the wall with one hand and the flashlight with the other, I slowly crept down the stairs. I didn't even realize I was holding my breath until I started getting dizzy.

"Pull it together, Rowan," I muttered under my breath. It had the intended effect, as I pulled my shoulders back and took another deep breath. Once I got to the bottom, I slowly waved the flashlight from side to side. Relieved to discover I was on my own in the tunnel, I moved forward slowly. About halfway between the two sets of stairs, I discovered more food wrappers and a dark green sweater. I picked up the sweater and was surprised by how luxurious it felt. This was some high-quality wool and, like the water bottle, had the distinct "feel" of money.

Someone must have left in a hurry, I surmised. Picking up the remaining wrappers, I turned back towards the entrance. No point attracting rodents with food waste, was my thinking.

I then had another thought that unnerved me. What if the person or persons who had been down here was indeed trying to access Black Thumb Betty's? The only way I'd know for sure was to inspect the top of the stairs that led into my shop. Not knowing what I would discover, I turned around yet again and headed further into the tunnel. At the bottom of the other stairs, I stopped to scan the walls and stairs before ascending. Nothing seemed out of the ordinary, so I started my ascent. I tossed the sweater and wrappers behind me, using my free hand to steady myself against the wall. I could pick them up on my way out.

At the top of the stairs leading into my shop, I sat down for a moment to catch my breath. I was still nervous about what I might discover, but I had come this far. Standing up, I turned around and directed the flashlight towards the now-sealed entrance. A gasp escaped my lips when I discovered that someone had indeed been trying to access the shop. There were scratch marks up and down the plaster that covered the door. But why, I pondered. Who could possibly want to access my shop uninvited after the village outcry to the last unwelcome entry?

How odd that the anonymous notes had arrived the night before hearing someone in the tunnel. Were they connected or was it just a case of bad timing? My brain was going a mile a minute as I tried to process this latest development. Just when I had started feeling safe and settled in the village, this had to happen. Now, I didn't know if my future here was secure.

I had slid down to sit on the top step once again, unaware that the dampness from the mossy stair was seeping through my pants. Shivering, I realized I needed to get back to the shop and warm up with a nice, hot cup of coffee and a dry pair of pants.

I retraced my steps, retrieving the fancy sweater and wrappers on the way. The conditions in the tunnel made it difficult to pick up the pace safely, but once I was back above ground, I would sprint back to the shop. That would help me warm up and distract my brain from the worst-case scenarios it was currently concocting.

Back on Sycamore Row, I headed to the external staircase that led directly to my suite above the shop. I was in need of a hot shower and a change of clothes before a hot coffee. Entering the suite, I could hear Cinnamon snoring. Snoring! That cat really was something else. I had been risking my life, and he was oblivious to it all. Maybe I'd warm myself up by cuddling up to him. He was a furnace after all. Shower first, I thought, as I shed my clothes and headed to the bathroom.

6

The sun was finally rising, and I had finished all the opening prep. I had stashed the sweater behind the front counter, which was now laden with carafes of my most popular sellers—namely, cardamom latte, hot coffee, and one of Betty's old standby beverages: cinnamon-cardamom herbal tea. All that was left was to unlock the door and put the sandwich board out front.

I had been playing around with different names on the temporary display board for a few weeks. But so far, none of my proposed name changes were receiving approval from customers. Not to mention Tilda and Cinnamon, who scoffed and hissed, respectively, at my attempts. Perhaps keeping the shop as Black Thumb Betty's was the continuity a small village like Cresswell-on-Wyrd craved. Some things were better left untouched, was Tilda's philosophy.

This morning, though, I had written a new message in chalk:

Sweater (jumper) found. Please inquire within.

I much preferred the American term but realized many Brits knew them only as jumpers, so opted to write both on the board. Maybe the culprit from the tunnel would reveal themselves by claiming their lost clothing. One could only hope.

Checking my watch, I decided to call Piper at Blooming Brews. She was an early riser and would have been prepping for her opening as well. I was excited to learn how the rest of the night had gone for Elspeth. Just as I picked up the phone, I heard the bell above the door chime. It was Piper, arriving in person to update me on her mother. Yet again, just thinking about someone conjured them. Shaking my head, I wondered if I'd ever get to the bottom of the odd happenings in this village.

"Piper! You must be psychic. I was just picking up the phone to call you."

Holding the phone to show her caused Piper to snort out a laugh. How odd, I thought. She reminded me of my dad when he laughed. More strange correlations for me to unpack, I realized, but they would have to wait.

"Oh, how funny is that?"

"Right? How did it go with Elspeth last night?"

Piper walked up to the counter and leaned against it. She looked tired but not as stressed as she had been the day before.

"Better than the last time. No visions of Cinnamon singing and dancing..."

"But? I feel like there's a but coming."

She nodded and looked down at her hands.

"Yes, there is a but. But she still didn't recognize Petunia or me."

I leaned forward and squeezed Piper's hands. It felt like

there was more to the story, but I didn't want to gloss over her disappointment.

"I'm sorry, Piper. This must be so tough for you. Did she remember anything?"

"Yes!" Piper seemed excited by my question. "She talked about her early work with Betty. That must have been before we were born."

I squeezed her hands again. This was progress, even if Piper didn't see it that way.

"Well, that's a start. I wonder if I increase the cloves even more..."

My brain was going a mile a minute. I ran around the desk and locked the door. We needed some uninterrupted time in the kitchen to work on a new blend. I waved towards Piper as I continued towards the swinging doors.

"Come on! Let's work on a new blend right now."

Excitedly, Piper raced after me, catching up to me before I entered the kitchen. My enthusiasm and willingness to include her in the research had given her hope. That was the next best thing to getting her mum's memories back.

We spent the next hour playing around with different formulations for Recollection Restorative. I packed up a thermos for Piper to take with her and walked her to the front door. She had specific instructions for administering it to her mother twice in the day: as soon as she saw her and then right before bed. We were cautiously optimistic that a double dose in an eight-or-so-hour window would be more effective than a single dose.

"I'll call or drop by tomorrow morning and update you on this latest blend."

Standing at the door, she reached over and pulled me into a hug. I laughed as I hugged her back, feeling her optimism bubbling over too.

"Sounds like a plan. Good luck, Piper."

Wandering back towards the kitchen, I greeted Cinnamon as he descended from our suite.

"Hello sleepyhead. I don't know about you, but I'm exhausted from our early-morning walk."

Yawning, I quietly hoped that the customers would be few and far between today. That way, I could hang out on the couch in the alcove, grabbing cat naps here and there. The bell above the door shattered my wishing spell. A few customers entered and headed straight to the counter. I had already turned towards them and didn't notice Cinnamon's reaction. He had turned in a huff towards the kitchen door.

I was busy for the rest of the day. Closing the shop for an hour that morning had spurred many villagers to drop by. I heard a few of them whispering that they thought the shop was again in trouble. My hope for a brief nap was dashed, as I was literally run off my feet for the rest of the day.

The sun was setting as I was finally able to close the shop. My early morning foray with Cinnamon, combined with a busy day, had me hopeful that I would sleep well that night. I was too tired to be hungry, so I decided to head to bed.

Just as I reached the staircase, I heard a tentative knock at the door. Sighing, I turned to see Ellie Place, wife of chemist Gideon, standing shyly outside the shop. I turned around and headed over to let her in.

"Ellie, hi. I'm sorry, I've closed for the day."

Waving my hand towards the counter, I continued.

"It was a crazy-busy day, and I'm sold out of everything. I'm so wiped out that I was just heading up to take my second shower of the day and go right to bed."

She alternated between glancing over her shoulder and looking down at her feet. Her nervousness was evident in her body language, and I immediately felt badly for shutting her down. I guided her towards the counter as I rushed over my words, hoping to make her feel at ease.

"I'm sure I could whip you up something yummy if you don't mind waiting a few minutes."

Finally, she spoke. "I, I, I'm sorry to bother you so late. I knew you were closed."

"Oh? What can I do for you?"

"Well, you see, Betty..."

This must have been one of those late-night visits Rory had mentioned when I first arrived in the village. Ellie seemed uncomfortable, so I jumped in to reassure her.

"Did Betty create something special for you?"

Nodding, she looked down at her feet. It was like pulling teeth to get her to share. I smiled so she would know that I was open to hearing her request.

"She, she made me something to calm my nerves. The children..."

Having four young children and an inattentive husband was clearly impacting Ellie. I could help her, but it couldn't be tonight. First, a review of *Betty's Steep Secrets* was in order. And possibly a consultation with Tilda, who knew Betty's cryptic code.

"I can help you, for sure, Ellie. But I'm afraid it'll have to wait until tomorrow. You see, I need to consult Betty's recipe book to see what she made for you. Are you okay to come back tomorrow?"

No sooner had I spoken when Gideon burst into the shop. His expression made me nervous, and I wasn't sure if he was angrier with me or his wife.

"Ellie! What are you doing here? I told you this place is full of mumbo jumbo."

He next turned his rage towards me.

"And you! I want you to stay away from my family. No good will come of your witch-adjacent behavior."

"Whoa, whoa, whoa. Cool your jets, man. Your wife came to me. I didn't lure her in here."

Just then, Cinnamon emerged from the kitchen. Although we'd had our differences earlier in the day, he immediately came to my defence. Placing himself between me and Gideon, Cinnamon started hissing at the man. It was like he was part cat, part guard dog, and I couldn't have been happier. Gideon jumped back, but his anger didn't subside. A man who always had to have the last word, he looked up at me.

"Regardless, I stand by what I said. This village would be better off without you."

And with that, he grabbed Ellie's arm and pulled her out the door.

I looked down and nodded at Cinnamon, who was still standing on guard.

"Thanks, pal. Appreciate your support."

He seemed indifferent to my thanks, but at least I knew he didn't hate me. Not like Gideon, at least. There was no love lost between Gideon and I, but I was beginning to wonder if he had sent me the anonymous note ordering me to leave the village. This latest confrontation had wound me up, and I wasn't sure I'd be able to sleep until I wrote some thoughts on paper. Getting them out of my head and into the world, that would help relax me before bed.

I wandered into the kitchen to retrieve my notebook. Cinnamon followed me and settled into his cat bed. Sitting at the table, I began a new list of suspects:

ANONYMOUS NOTE WRITER: suspects

1. Hortense Slack
2. Gideon Place
3. Whoever left the sweater in the tunnel
4. Clive Smeaton and/or Chase & Hunter Smeaton

Granted, that last entry was a bit of a stretch. Although, we had made our peace at the end of the last Village Council meeting, I still felt some animosity from my next-door business neighbors. Their father Clive was adamant that sons Chase and Hunter stay in the village to help him run Smeaton & Sons Butchery. The sons, on the other hand, wanted to fly the coop and chase trends in London.

Just writing this list had eased my mind substantially. Suddenly, I felt a wave of exhaustion pass over me. It was time to hit the hay, no second shower needed. All of this could wait until the morning.

7

Wednesday
Three Days Before the Great Harvest Bake Off

It had been a terrible night. Our early-morning escapades had not helped me fall asleep. If anything, I had tossed and turned more than ever. Maybe creating that list of suspects hadn't been such a great idea after all. Instead of easing my mind, it had brought it to the forefront. Every dried leaf crunching under shoes, every branch lashing against a building, all of it scared the wits out of me, certain that someone was trying to break into the shop.

I groaned as I got out of bed and headed to the shower. Perhaps a cold dose of water rushing over my body would jolt me awake. If not, there was always coffee, and I was definitely looking forward to the first sip this morning. When I headed down to the shop, I wanted to call Piper right away and see how Elspeth's evening and night had gone. Hopefully, the adjusted Recollection Restorative blend had brought her memory recall into the current decade. Better yet, the current year.

Cinnamon was nowhere to be found when I returned to my room to get dressed. I suspected he had slept in his cat bed downstairs. When I entered the kitchen, my suspicions were confirmed. Cinnamon lifted his head when he heard me, then yawned, and returned his head to its position on his front paw. He wrapped his tail around his head, shielding his eyes from the light, and me. It looked like we wouldn't be sharing any conversation this morning. That was fine with me, as I was so tired I couldn't think straight. And I still needed to consult with Tilda about the cardamom losing its effect on Cinnamon. But that could wait until after coffee and a call to Piper.

I finished my coffee in the kitchen, wary to be seen in the shop before I was ready to interact with anyone. The morning opening routine was definitely becoming second nature to me. Running on autopilot, it was only when I scalded my hand against the teapot that I noticed I was brewing tea. Shaking my head to refocus, I picked up the carafes that were ready for customers and headed out front. I'd return for the cinnamon-cardamom tea later.

While I was heading to the counter, I heard the bell chime and looked towards the door. Arthur and Tilda were standing outside the shop, with large smiles and a bristling energy between them that was palpable even through the closed door. Love definitely seemed to be in the air this fine morning. Instead of leaning on his cane, which was firmly tucked under his other arm, Arthur was leaning on Tilda. She seemed only too happy with the physical contact.

I set down the carafes and opened the door for my friends. Tilda was positively effusive as she greeted me.

"Rowan, darling! I'm so sorry for my absence these past few days."

Arthur chuckled as Tilda led him to the couch in the front alcove. "Yes, I'm afraid I'm to blame for that. I was so enjoying Tilda's company."

I held up the carafe of coffee and received nods from both of them. It was early enough in the morning for my second cup, so I prepared three mugs and carried them on a tray to the alcove.

"Well, you're here now and that's all that matters. But Arthur, I saw Rory a few days ago, and he mentioned the two of you were heading to London. Yesterday."

Tilda's entire body vibrated as she giggled. Yes, love was definitely in the air.

"Pish posh. I'm the boss and I decided to stay. And that's all I have to say on the matter."

"Okay then! Case closed." I chuckled nervously, surprised by Arthur's outburst.

The entire mood of the shop had lifted with their arrival, and I welcomed the distraction from everything swirling around in my head. We spent the next while catching up and easing into the day with our coffees. Even though I hadn't seen Tilda for half a week, it felt like forever. She had been a daily presence in my life, until she wanted physical space between her and former landlord, Gideon. I couldn't blame her, but she would have to face him eventually. Cresswell-on-Wyrd was a small village, and their paths would cross sooner or later. In the meantime, I was just happy to have her back in the shop.

Before Arthur left us, he asked to have a word in private. Tilda took that opportunity to head to the restroom. He leaned forward on the couch, whispering so quietly, I had to lean forward in my chair to hear him.

"I can't emphasize enough how important it is to keep my potential retirement under wraps."

Arthur's reminder of his secret brought me back to how many I was actually keeping: his from Rory, Rory's from him, and the whole cat-talking situation from the entire village. Suddenly, my shoulders felt the weight of these secrets, and I slumped back in my chair. Arthur looked concerned when he saw my reaction, but his response indicated he had misinterpreted my behavior.

"What's wrong? Have you spilled the beans already?"

Part of me wanted to laugh at him, but one glance at his face and I knew that would go over as well as a lead balloon.

"No, no, it's not that at all. Of course I'm keeping it to myself."

Arthur leaned back himself, clearly relieved by my continued discretion. But he kept prodding me about my demeanor, which wasn't helping me keep Rory's secret to myself. It was this type of situation that stressed me out when it came to maintaining others' confidences. I was equally disappointed and unsurprised that, as a lawyer, he would continue to pester someone who wasn't being forthcoming.

"Then what has caused such a visceral backlash to my words?"

How could I answer him without revealing what I knew? Just then, Cinnamon made his presence known, meowing and yawning simultaneously as he arrived through the cat door that led to the kitchen. That was it! I'd focus on Cinnamon's secret. I walked over and picked him up before I spoke up. It was a ploy on my part to shift Arthur's penetrating gaze from my face and buy me some time.

"Just feeling a bit overwhelmed about keeping secrets. There's yours, this guy's," I scratched Cinnamon's ears and was rewarded with a purring chirp, "not to mention the Catmint Council. And the latter two require me to deceive my customers on a regular basis."

Arthur stood and ambled towards us, leaning heavily on his cane as he walked. He patted Cinnamon's head before comforting me with a gentle shoulder squeeze.

"I understand your concern, Rowan. And if the village knew about Cinnamon, that would certainly eliminate the need for the Catmint Council."

Placing Cinnamon on the ground, I clapped my hands together.

"That's it! We should come clean at the next Village Council meeting. Then that's two secrets I no longer have to keep."

Two down, two to go, I thought to myself. Better than none down, I supposed.

"Woah, Nelly. Hold your horses, young lady."

Arthur raised his hands as he spoke, dropping his cane to the ground. I reached down to retrieve it, crossing the fingers on my other hand behind my back. Rather than look at him, I kept my head down as I handed him the fallen cane. My worry was that my face would reveal my thoughts and he'd figure out that I was keeping other secrets too. I was partially saved by Tilda's return, as she rushed over to help steady Arthur. He waved her away and hobbled under his own power back to the couch. Once seated, he smiled warmly at both of us before addressing Tilda.

"Would you mind terribly ringing Rory to bring the car around? I'm not sure these old legs can handle the walk home."

Tilda rushed towards the phone so quickly, she looked like a movie being fast-forwarded. Arthur's wish was indeed her command. I motioned towards the kitchen and pointed at Cinnamon, resulting in nods from both visitors. The cat bowls needed to be cleaned out and replaced with fresh food and water. And I wanted to get a new batch of cardamom latte steeping on the oven. My extended stay in the kitchen was also a ruse to allow the lovebirds more one-on-one time before Arthur's next trip into London. I knew Tilda would join me in the kitchen once Rory arrived to pick up Arthur.

"Okay, my feline friend. I've had my morning coffee and I'm ready to continue our experiments. Tilda is back in the shop, so she and I can take turns serving customers while the other stays back here with you."

I had so much to share with Tilda—the two anonymous notes, the curious discovery in the secret tunnel, the latest rounds of Recollection Restorative with Elspeth, and the waning effects of cardamom on Cinnamon's ability to speak. In spite of the growing list of mysteries to crack, I was excited to dive in.

8

Tilda joined me in the kitchen after Arthur departed. Her face was positively glowing but, as much as I wanted to know more about her feelings for Arthur, I also wanted to respect her space and allow this blooming romance to grow organically. Rather than pester her for details, I decided to wait until she broached the topic.

"That smells divine. What delicious beverage are you concocting this morning?"

Tilda walked over to the stove, leaning towards the gently boiling liquid. She used her hand to waft the rising steam towards her nose, inhaling appreciatively as she did.

"As I suspected, cardamom on its own is losing effectiveness for Cinnamon. And catmint is not an option, unless we want Cinnamon singing and dancing all around the village."

Tilda's giggle was bubbly and light, spilling over like champagne fizz. "No, we don't want that to happen. At least not in public. So what is your plan?"

I walked towards the kitchen table, pulling open the drawer to retrieve the anonymous notes I had received the night before. Holding them up, I sat down at the table and waved to the seat across for Tilda. She completed one quick stir of the brewing cardamom latte before joining me.

Filling her in on the first note, I passed it over as I explained my new theory. "This burnt page was clearly written by Aunt Betty."

Tilda nodded in agreement. "Yes, I recognize Betty's handwriting. But I don't recall this, 'To remember what I knew, you must trust the spice that opens the tongue.' It must be from before my time."

"It's possible that Betty worked on it when Elspeth was helping her in the shop."

"You know about Elspeth's time in the shop? Did the Bloom girls—ahem, women—tell you that?" My narrowed eyes when Tilda referred to the almost-thirty-year-old twins as girls caused her to correct herself mid-sentence.

"Actually, it was Cinnamon who told me about that. So, I decided to increase the amount of ground cloves in Recollection Restorative and see what happens. That's what we gave to Elspeth yesterday."

Glancing at my watch, I remembered that I was about to check in with Piper when Arthur and Tilda had arrived. The fact that she hadn't yet called had me cautiously optimistic that the latest formulation had worked with little to no side effects.

Looking up, I could see that Tilda was waiting to be filled in on the latest experiment, so I did just that. Discussion about the other note could wait.

At the end of my explanation, Tilda's recap left me feeling self-conscious about experimenting on my own. "No catmint and loads of cloves. Is that all you did to change it up this time? We don't want to modify too many ingredients at once. If we do that, we won't know which change actually worked."

"Fair point, but I figure the decrease/increase are really one step."

Tilda tilted her head questioningly, urging me to continue. "How so?"

"Removing the catmint takes us back to the original version of cardamom latte, and we know the cardamom isn't working on its own anymore. So, that particular blend is off the table for now. Next step is to basically increase other herbs and test their effectiveness. If the results are questionable, we can next look at lowering the amount of cardamom."

As I spoke, I reached into the drawer again. This time, I pulled out *Betty's Steep Secrets*, my aunt's cryptic recipe book. Turning towards the end of the book, I lifted it up to show Tilda my latest entries: Cardamom Latte for Cat Speech. Although I was continuing my aunt's rigorous note-taking during herbal-based research, I had declined to learn her cryptic code. Instead, I was writing everything in plain old English, for ease of reference. I wasn't nearly as paranoid as my aunt was, at least not about this book being stolen or tampered with again.

No, I had other things to worry me.

The bell above the shop entrance tinkled, and Tilda hopped out of her chair to serve the new customers. I reached out and grabbed the burnt page, slipping it into the recipe book and leaving the other anonymous note on the table. We had yet to discuss its appearance, possible suspects, and my unnerving discovery in the tunnel.

The bell chimed again, and I heard several more voices out front. My discussions with Tilda would have to wait, as it was shaping up to be another busy day at Black Thumb Betty's.

Before joining her out front, I wandered over to the stove. Once the burner was off, I moved the hot pot to a trivet on the table. I would refrigerate this batch when it was cool enough. It was time to experiment with iced drink versions, I decided right then and there. The bell chimed another time, and I hurried to join Tilda in the shop. Further experiments with new beverage concoctions would have to wait until tomorrow.

A steady flow of customers kept us busy for the rest of the morning, but it was a welcome respite from my overactive brain and tired body. I didn't have time to worry about anything at all; I was too busy pouring drinks, ringing in sales, and running back to the kitchen to restock the empty carafes. By lunchtime, the rush was over and both Tilda and I collapsed on the couch. After yesterday's early morning walk with Cinnamon, subsequent sleuthing in the tunnel, and last night's terrible sleep, I was struggling to keep my eyes open.

"Dear, you look like you're going to pass out right here. Why don't you pop upstairs for a lie down? I'll hold down the fort while you get some of your prized 'cave' time.'"

Yawning, I stretched my arms over my head as I stood up. I didn't need to be asked twice. Before heading to the staircase near the kitchen door, I popped into the kitchen. The new version of cardamom latte had cooled to room temperature, and I wanted to take a glass upstairs with me. Popping in some ice cubes to cool it down even further, I grabbed my glass in one hand, using the other to open the fridge and place the cooled teapot inside. Back in the shop, I reached the stairs and then realized I hadn't responded to Tilda. I turned and smiled at her.

"Thank you, I think I will. Please come yell in my ear if I'm not back in two hours."

"I will do no such thing. But I may jiggle your shoulder gently."

I chuckled at Tilda's reaction to my suggestion. She was definitely not the yelling type, which was one of the reasons I found her so endearing. Making a mental note to discuss with her the other anonymous letter I had received, I fell asleep as soon as my head hit the pillow.

9

After my midday nap, I awoke feeling rested and refreshed. Checking my watch, I chuckled to myself. Tilda had indeed allowed me to sleep longer than two hours. And I suspected she hadn't even attempted to jiggle my shoulder at the two-hour mark.

Looking down, I saw that Cinnamon was curled up at my feet. The ice cubes had melted while I slept, and my once-hot cardamon latte was now room temperature again, but still delicious. I took a few sips from the glass I'd left on my bedside table, then leaned down to offer some to Cinnamon. He awoke immediately when I placed my latte-dripping finger under his nose. As soon as he smelled the latest blend, he swatted my hand away and stomped out of the bedroom.

"Hey! That was rude. I was just trying to offer you some of my latte."

He wasn't having any of it, so I gave up trying to reason with him. As I headed towards the stairs that would take me back down to the shop, I heard voices below. It was an animated discussion, with at least three distinct females in the mix.

My assessment had been correct—the voices I had heard belonged to Tilda, Piper, and Elspeth. Surprisingly, it was Elspeth who was dominating the conversation. She sounded lucid and engaged. Judging by the looks on Tilda and Piper's faces, her demeanor was a welcome change. Piper glanced my way and smiled—a gesture that lit up her entire face. She waved me over to join their conversation at the counter.

"Rowan! My mother was just singing your praises."

Elspeth turned towards me and smiled too. Her smile didn't reach her eyes like Piper's had, and I could tell she didn't recognize me. I wasn't concerned, as she'd only known me for a very short while. In helping to find the right formulation of Recollection Restorative, my goal was for her to recognize her daughters. She looked at Piper to acknowledge her comment, and I was delighted to see awareness in her expression. I joined them at the counter as I responded to Piper's comment.

"What have I done to earn your praise, Elspeth?"

"Piper tells me you've been helping her with my memory. I woke up this morning after an incredibly refreshing sleep."

"It's true. Petunia and I normally take turns getting up in the night with Mum. She rarely sleeps through the night anymore. Last night, neither of us had to check on her."

This was definitely an intriguing development. I pondered to myself if the Recollection Restorative was more of a sleep aid, and that was what had influenced her memory recall. Lost in thought, the conversation continued without me for a spell.

I made a mental note to try this herbal tea blend with

Reverend Primrose. Perhaps it would work better than the Sleep Salve, and without the bizarre side effects. Hearing my name brought me back to the present.

"Hmmm? Sorry, I zoned out momentarily. What was that, Piper?"

"I was just wondering what you changed with this latest batch of Recollection Restorative. As you can see, it seems to have worked for Mum's memory. She knew both of us this morning, and she was much more interactive than she has been in a long time."

"Well, the first step was to remove the catmint. That particular herb impacts people in similar ways, regardless of the other ingredients or method of delivery. Next, I added ground cloves to the..." I stopped mid-sentence, when I realized that Elspeth was muttering under her breath. "I'm sorry, did you just say 'clove conspiracy'?"

My pointed question caught her off guard and she began pacing the floor. Pulling at her auburn hair, her face revealed the dramatic tug of war playing out in her head. Finally, she stopped pacing and stood directly in front of me.

"You added cloves to the herbal blend?"

"That's right," I nodded, "what is it about cloves that made you say 'clove conspiracy'?"

"Did you know I used to help Betty with her experiments?"

I looked towards Tilda and Piper, who were hanging on Elspeth's every word. We all nodded in unison, quietly urging her to continue. Sensing she had the floor—and our undivided attention—Elspeth twirled around before speaking again. Nervous reaction, I surmised, but kept quiet to give her space to gather her thoughts. After a second twirl, she steadied herself and finally spoke.

"Cloves were a staple in Betty's early work with Cinnamon."

The plot thickened as awareness dawned on me that Elspeth too knew about Cinnamon's ability to speak.

"It had a very specific purpose too. We wanted to suppress his early memories. When Betty rescued him from the RSPCA, the staff indicated that his first year of life wasn't a pleasant one. We called it the Clove Conspiracy, because we were keeping the true purpose of that specific formulation from him."

I heard an aggressive meow behind me. Turning my head, I noticed that Cinnamon had followed me down after our nap. In addition to his meow, Cinnamon shuddered at Elspeth's comment. Because of his reaction, I knew that, after today, we would never speak of this again.

"That explains so much. Thank you for telling me, Elspeth."

Since everyone present already knew about Cinnamon's speaking ability, I felt comfortable addressing him directly.

"Cinnamon, you have my word. I will never knowingly expose you to cloves again. Having said that, I will still be using it in various beverages for the shop."

"And herbal-based remedies," Piper chimed in.

I pointed towards her and nodded in agreement.

"That too. So, please don't sample anything without checking with Tilda or I first."

If I had to guess, I would have said that Cinnamon was equal parts miffed and relieved. He walked to the centre of our group and took turns walking up to each of us. He hissed at Elspeth, turned towards me and hissed again. With Tilda and Piper he was gentler: each received a pat on the foot with his front paw. Finished rendering his assessments of the assembled women, Cinnamon turned and skulked off to the kitchen.

Everyone stayed quiet for a moment, unsure what to say. I decided to break the awkward silence.

"I think he needs some time to process this."

The other three lowered their heads and nodded solemnly. We were all feeling guilty that Cinnamon had to discover the truth in this very public way. He was likely in his cat bed, licking his wounds and reflecting on memories lost.

Suddenly, Elspeth reached out to steady herself against the counter. She appeared flushed and somewhat confused. Looking around, she seemed to be registering her surroundings for the first time. I wondered if the Recollection Restorative was finally wearing off. Or perhaps she was getting sleepy and needed to rest. My gut was telling me that Betty's herbal-based remedies didn't actually do what we all thought they did. At least not for humans.

Piper noticed her mother's confused look and put her arm around her shoulder. Tilda rushed forward to open the door for them, as Piper led her mother towards the sidewalk.

"Okay Mum. This has been a very eventful day for you. Let's get you home so you can rest. Petunia can close up the shop on her own."

Piper waved over her head as they continued outside. We both yelled goodbye before Tilda closed and locked the door. She moved towards the front alcove. Sitting down on the couch, she patted the seat beside her.

"Well, let's have a good old catchup before any more customers disturb us."

"Give me two secs. I want to get a few things from the kitchen."

And with that, I dashed off to retrieve the anonymous note from the table as well as Betty's—now my—recipe book. Out of breath when I returned, I flopped on the couch beside Tilda. She giggled and patted my arm.

"I'll let you catch your breath. Now show me what you've got in your hand."

I pushed the note towards her but hung on to the recipe book. In my mind, that threat was the priority to discuss and, with any luck, determine the sender or senders. Tilda gasped when she read it, covering her mouth with her other hand in the process. I could tell she was as shocked as I had been when I first read it.

"'*Leave now. You're not wanted here.*' That sounds so ominous. Oh, Rowan."

Tilda leaned over and enveloped me in a hug I didn't even know I needed. But her comfort helped calm my racing heart. I could feel my shoulders releasing some of the tension I'd been holding these past few days. Before I knew it, I was crying on Tilda's shoulder.

"There, there, dear. This is a lot to bear on your own."

She pulled me away from her, grasping me by each shoulder. Our faces were mere inches apart. She waited until I was looking directly into her eyes before she spoke.

"I'm so sorry I've been preoccupied with Arthur. Please, next time you need me, just call and snap me out of my foolishness."

I nodded, sniffling because I didn't feel like I could speak yet without the waterworks erupting again. A few deep breaths and I finally felt like I could respond.

"You and Arthur seemed really happy, and I didn't want to intrude."

"Poppycock! We're just two silly old fools. Intrude away.

I'm sure he'll be heading into London today, and you'll have me to yourself."

"That sounds nice. I could use some help. Not just with this crazy note but also helping sort out Cinnamon. As infuriating as he is sometimes, I want to help him have more control over his ability to speak."

"You have my word we'll get a more permanent solution for Cinnamon. But, first, I want to hear your theories on this note."

I leaned back on the couch, pulling my list out from the book.

ANONYMOUS NOTE WRITER: suspects

1. Hortense Slack
2. Gideon Place
3. Whoever left the sweater in the tunnel
4. Clive Smeaton and/or Chase & Hunter Smeaton

After walking her through everything that had happened to get me to this point, she looked again at the list.

"I agree with your assessment. It could be any one of these individuals. Do you have a gut feeling about who it might be?"

I titled my head until it was resting on the back of the couch, closing my eyes to focus. Who might it be? Who indeed. Before I could respond, Tilda jumped in again.

"It could also be someone else entirely."

She wasn't wrong, but that was not what I wanted to hear. Groaning, I opened my eyes and looked at her.

"Is there something you want to tell me?"

"Arthur and I ate at the Hare & Harrow recently."

I grabbed Tilda's arm, causing her to stop speaking. She had been across the road from my shop and hadn't popped in to say hello! Judging from the look on her face, Tilda could tell she'd hurt my feelings. She backpedaled immediately before continuing with her theory.

"We tried to pop in and say hello, but the shop was locked up tight. All the lights were out."

"That must have been when I went to Blooming Brews to deliver the new batch of Recollection Restorative."

Relieved that I hadn't been completely abandoned, I smiled at my flighty friend. She took that as encouragement to continue.

"Moira was out at the time, something about a bridge tournament in the next village. Her grandson, Lewis," at the mention of his name, we both shuddered. The sweaty and stocky man was a transplant to COW who hadn't grown up in the village. Lewis had not endeared himself to anyone since arriving. "He was bragging behind the bar."

"Bragging about what?"

"Well, I couldn't catch it all, but I distinctly heard him say Black Magic Betty."

It was a term that had been bandied about when I first arrived in the village. I had hosted a grand reopening, called the Cuppa Comeback. Much chaos had ensued when Arthur arrived after being locked in his car by Petunia. It was also the day Cinnamon had barked like a dog in front of young Tilly Place. Someone who had been in attendance had started the whisper campaign that same evening at the Hare & Harrow.

"A gossipy term that I thought I had overcome. Sheesh, don't these people have anything better to do with their lives."

My last statement caught me off guard. Maybe I wasn't

suited to village life after all. Of course, my neighbors really had nothing better to do; we were living in a small, quiet village where everyone seemed to know everyone else's business. It was as if gossip was the currency of choice. And me, as a newcomer, was ripe for the picking. Tilda snapped her fingers in front of my face to bring me back to the present moment.

"Rowan, I know Cresswell-on-Wyrd is no Brooklyn, but people don't mean you any harm."

Holding up the anonymous note, I challenged Tilda's assessment.

"Don't they? I mean, come on, this note just sounds..." I was wracking my brain for just the right descriptor, "... ominous. Yes, that's it. It sounds ominous. Threatening, really."

Tilda sighed and threw her hands up in the air. She knew it was a lost cause to try and change my mind. Instead, she reached forward and plucked my list of suspects off the table where I had tossed it. Scrutinizing the list again, she asked for a pen. I handed her the one that slipped into a tidy elastic along the edge of Betty's—my—recipe book. Leaning forward to write required an uncrossing of her legs.

ANONYMOUS NOTE WRITER: suspects

1. Hortense Slack
2. ~~Gideon Place~~
3. Whoever left the sweater in the tunnel
4. ~~Clive Smeaton and/or~~ Chase & Hunter Smeaton
5. Lewis Culpepper

Tilda crossed out Gideon and Clive but added Lewis to

the mix. I looked at her questioningly, waiting for her explanation.

"I think Gideon and Clive learned their lesson when they tried to push through Clive's plans to take over the space occupied by Black Thumb Betty's. Though there's no love lost, I don't think they would threaten you in this way."

I wasn't sure how I felt about Tilda eliminating them from my list. Pondering it for a moment, I decided to give her the benefit of the doubt. "I suppose that makes sense. Though my last encounter with Gideon was still fraught with bitterness."

"Honestly, I think he's more upset with me. But since we haven't been in contact since I moved out, he likely views you as a suitable replacement for his rancor."

Before I could respond, a commotion outside the shop drew our attention away from my list. Looking up, a gasp escaped my lips. My father, Reginald Thorne, was standing on the sidewalk. The leashes from his sibling pugs, Pudding and Pickles, were twisted around the legs of Chase Smeaton. His brother, Hunter, was jumping up and down, laughing uncontrollably.

10

I rushed outside, not even noticing if Tilda had followed me.

"Dad! What the heck? You said you were coming next month."

My father glanced up at me and broke out into the biggest smile. Forgetting about the dogs, he dropped both leashes and embraced me in a hug. I hadn't realized how much I had missed him until that moment. But our reunion was short-lived, as we heard a car screech to a halt on Sycamore Row. One of the pugs had taken advantage of the loosened leash and run into the street.

The quick actions of the driver ensured no animals or people were harmed. But the scene outside my shop was chaotic nonetheless.

Releasing me from his hug, my dad raced into the street to pick up Pudding—or was it Pickles?—I couldn't tell them apart. He snorted as he laughed and I shook my head at the familiarity of the sound. It must be an English thing, I thought.

I picked up the leash for the other dog and gently tugged

it to keep them from following my dad into the street. Looking over at Chase and Hunter, I could see that Chase was turning the same shade of red as his brother's sweater. His brother's complexion was heading in that direction too. Though, Hunter's was from laughter and Chase's was purely from embarrassment. I smiled and waved towards them, hoping there were no hard feelings.

The brothers' reaction to me was almost comical in its simultaneousness. It was as if a giant eraser had been slid down their faces. Their expressions turned dour and, as one, they spun on their heels and retreated into Smeaton & Sons Butchery. It reinforced to me their position on my suspect list, and I shelved that thought until Tilda and I could continue our discussion.

My father had finally returned to the sidewalk, and Tilda was now standing beside me with a joyous smile lighting up her entire face. She clapped her hands and reached forward, compelling me to deliver Pudding or Pickles into her arms.

"Aren't you the most scrumptious little creature ever!"

The pug lapped up the attention, while his/her sibling looked on from my father's arms. A whimper drew Tilda's attention to the other pooch. She opened her arms to welcome the dog, and my father obliged her. Tilda's face was awash in slobbery kisses from two very happy canines. My father reached down and enveloped me in another hug, causing me to laugh and cry all at once.

"Hello, dear girl. I'm so happy to see you."

I hugged him back fiercely before responding, worried my voice might crack. "Me too, Dad, me too."

Breaking free, I looked down at my father's luggage. He was definitely travelling light, with just a dog carrier and a small rolling suitcase.

"Is that all you have in the way of luggage, Dad?"

"Yes! Are you surprised at how light I'm travelling?"

"Very surprised. Wow, if Mom could see you now."

Mentioning my mother caused me to weep openly. The weight of my current challenges was making me overly emotional, something I tried to curtail on a daily basis. While I was still immensely sad that my mother wasn't here, I felt incredibly relieved that I could now lean on my father. He had already grabbed me in another hug. Turning me towards the shop, he deftly maneuvered me and his suitcase through the door. Tilda followed with both pugs in her arms and their carrier pushed along by one of her feet.

"No sense advertising your emotions to the entire village."

I laughed at my father's turn of phrase and felt better at once. Removing his hand from my shoulder, I squeezed it and let it fall. My face needed some TLC from a tissue, so I headed to the counter to retrieve a few.

The commotion in the shop brought Cinnamon into the fray. As soon as he saw the pugs in Tilda's arms, a hiss escaped his lips. Pudding and Pickles started squirming, desperate to sniff their fellow four-legged creature. Tilda obliged, putting them both on the ground and undoing their leashes. As one, they scurried towards the cat, much to his chagrin. His back reared up, a line of fur down his spine standing on end.

"Here's hoping the claws stay sheathed," my father snorted out a laugh and, again, I was taken aback by how much he resembled others in the village in that moment. Was it that English mannerism, not to mention hair, eyebrows, facial expression that made me think of the Bloom twins? Another mystery to add to my list, I decided.

I walked towards the animals, careful to avoid stepping

on any fast-moving body parts. Cinnamon was still holding his defensive position, but the pugs didn't seem bothered in the least. I hadn't expected my father and the pugs for at least a few more weeks, so I hadn't had time to prepare Cinnamon for their arrival either. This was his space, and he was definitely on the back foot.

The pugs were sniffing and panting, running around Cinnamon with tiny tails wagging furiously. The scene was bordering on comical, and we couldn't help ourselves from laughing at Cinnamon's predicament. I reached down to retrieve Cinnamon, who immediately leaned into my chest. His heart was racing from the encounter, so I stroked his head and whispered in his ear.

"Why don't you escape up to the suite. I'll secure the door so these two can't follow you. And don't worry, they're not staying here."

He placed a paw on my wrist, his signal that he agreed with my suggestion. Once he was safely ensconced upstairs, I turned to my father.

"Do you have food for these two? I can set up some bowls in the kitchen for them. They should be able to get through the cat door on their own."

My father reached into the side pocket of the dog carrier and pulled out a travel container. Shaking it drew both dogs to his feet, yipping in anticipation. He tossed it to me and pointed in my direction. Pudding and Pickles turned as one and raced towards me as fast as their little legs could carry them. Laughing, I waved them towards the kitchen, holding the swinging door open for them to pass through.

After getting them set up with food and water, I returned to the shop. Tilda and my father were chatting in the front alcove as if they had known each other for years. I was relieved that the two most important people in my life seemed to be getting along with no drama. I flopped down beside my dad, leaning my head against his shoulder.

"I'm so happy you're here, Dad. But you're early. You said you weren't coming until next month."

My comment produced another snorting laugh from my father, which got Tilda giggling uncontrollably. Both sounds were infectious and I found myself chuckling away.

"Oh, Rowan. You always were bad with dates. It *is* next month."

The confused look on my face was all my father needed to continue.

"I called you at the end of October. And now, it's the start of November. Hence, next month."

Slapping my head, I sighed and laughed at my own befuddlement.

"Of course, silly me. So, I guess you two introduced yourselves."

"That we did, dear. Tilda here has been filling me in on the drama surrounding your arrival and the shop. You've had quite the adventure."

"You don't know the half of it."

I wasn't ready to reveal the latest challenges to my father. At least not until he'd gotten settled and we'd had a chance to catch up. But my plans were dashed when he noticed the list on the table. Picking it up, he glanced at it before looking down at me.

"What's this? You've been receiving anonymous notes? Please explain."

The jig was up, so I filled him in on everything I had shared with Tilda. His reaction was classic Reginald Thorne.

"If there ever was a pearl-clutching moment, this is it."

"Oh, Dad. It's not that bad."

"Well, it's not great. Those two young men who got caught up in Pickles and Pudding's leashes, are they on this list?"

Nodding, I pointed to number four, where Tilda had crossed out Clive but kept Chase and Hunter.

"They think I'm keeping them from realizing their dream of opening a vegetarian barbecue bistro."

"Vegetarian BBQ? How preposterous."

I shrugged, not sure how to respond. Who was I to rain on their parade? If they thought a vegetarian barbecue could survive in Cresswell-on-Wyrd, well, more power to them. But I was not going to roll over and let them have the space Black Thumb Betty's had occupied for decades. Instead, I decided to focus on practical matters.

"You must be exhausted. Why don't we wander across the way to the Hare & Harrow to find you a room. Tilda, would you mind holding down the fort?"

Tilda was already standing, waving us towards the door.

"Go, go. I will do more than hold down the fort. I will also snuggle these delicious pooches."

Grabbing my father's hand, I pulled him off the couch and out the door that Tilda was now holding open for us. We would have time to catch up after he was settled.

11

I got my father settled in at the Hare & Harrow's sparse yet reasonably priced room above the pub. Although the sign out front said "pub and coaching inn", the inn portion was, in fact, just one room upstairs. Thankfully, for us, the room was not currently occupied. As such, Moira grudgingly agreed to allow Pickles and Pudding, my father's beloved pugs, to stay with him.

Saying goodbye to my father, I eased the door closed and tiptoed away. He was asleep before his head even hit the pillow. Determined to get back to the shop and confer with Tilda, I was taken aback when I heard a grunt and a sneer behind me.

Turning around, I saw Lewis Culpepper, Moira's cringe-worthy grandson making faces behind my back. I always tried to see the best in people, but Lewis made it difficult. Every interaction with this man had been uncomfortable, starting with the time he leaned against Cinnamon's back-pack carrier to breathe down my neck.

Today was no exception. He didn't stop making faces at me, even when I caught him in the act. Instead, he doubled down on his odious behavior with some choice insults thrown my way.

"Oh look, Black Magic Betty's evil spawn is gracing us with her presence."

No longer sure that his bark was mightier than his bite, I debated with myself before finally addressing his aggressive comment. I knew I would kick myself if I left without saying anything. And Tilda had convinced me that he could possibly be behind the threatening anonymous note. Ambling up to the bar, Lewis's face paled ever so slightly when he realized I wouldn't run away from his taunts.

"I hear you've been talking smack about me and my shop. Not to mention my dead Aunt Betty."

He sneered again before responding.

"Call a spade a spade, that's my philosophy. What of it? Are you going to go crying to Village Council again?"

"No, I am not. I don't really care what you say about me. It just shows your immaturity. But speaking ill of the dead, well, that's just cruel. And pathetic. Yes, that's what you are, Lewis. You're pathetic, attacking someone who can't defend themselves."

Lewis started sputtering at my critique of his behavior.

"Oh yeah? Well, your aunt was a crotchety old witch. The village is better off without her."

There would be no reasoning with him, so I decided to call it a day and head back to the safety and security of my own shop. The sad little man that he was, he heckled me one last time. I paid him no attention and continued on my way.

"Ooooh, the mighty American is running away with her tail between her legs. Can't handle a little British ribbing. How sad for her."

Even after the pub door slammed shut behind me, I

could still hear Lewis's taunts. Shaking my head, I checked for cars and bicycles before dashing across Sycamore Row. Just beyond Black Thumb Betty's, I could see Tilda wrestling both dog leashes as Pudding and Pickles yipped and yapped, running around her legs. The chaos of the moment wasn't lost on Tilda, who was giggling at her predicament. I picked up my pace and caught up with them in mere seconds, just in time to rescue her from a leash-inducing fall.

Tilda leaned against the window of Smeaton & Sons, handing me both leashes while she caught her breath. She placed her hand against her chest, taking deep breaths in an effort to slow down her breathing. I leaned over and scratched both pooches under the chin, gently commanding them to sit and stay. They happily obliged, their curlicue tails wagging a mile a minute.

"Rowan! Your timing is impeccable. We were just returning from a walk and bathroom break."

"That was great thinking, Tilda. I'm so used to Cinnamon sorting himself out with the litter box, I forgot that dogs need to be taken outside for nature breaks."

Tilda chuckled awkwardly at my mention of Cinnamon.

"Yes, well, our walk was precipitated by Cinnamon's arrival in the kitchen. It turns out these precious creatures had taken up residence in Cinnamon's cat bed, and he was none too pleased."

I cringed at the thought of flying fur and hurt feelings.

"Was it bad? I hope none of them were injured in the scuffle."

"No scuffle, thankfully. Just hissing from Cinnamon and frightened yips from these two as they awoke."

Wiping the back of my hand across my forehead to indicate relief, I turned back towards the shop. Tilda followed me, but not too closely. I suspected she was worried about getting tangled in the leashes again. At her age, a fall could be downright life-altering.

Once inside the shop, I untethered Pudding and Pickles. Another command to sit and stay yielded the desired results.

"Thank goodness my father trained these two. Now, I'll run upstairs and fetch a blanket. We can use it to fashion a little bed for them in the front alcove."

"Excellent idea, Rowan. That should keep them out of Cinnamon's hair. I mean, fur."

Tilda laughed at her own joke. Personally, I groaned as I made my way to the secret staircase.

Once the dogs were settled on the blanket, I turned back to the shop door and flipped the sign from closed to open.

"I'm not even sure why I keep this sign here. If the door is locked, everyone seems to bang on it until I open it for them. If I'm here, that is."

"Yes, Cresswellians are a demanding bunch. They want their tea or coffee when it suits them."

Tilda's interpretation of running a business always made me shake my head. I wondered if she had been so resolute about opening and closing hours when she was serving as the village's pharmacist.

"In America, it goes without saying that you post your opening hours and then stick to them."

"Every day?"

"Every day."

It was Tilda's turn to shake her head as she absorbed my comments.

"We do things differently in British villages. Most customers are also friends and neighbors, so they understand if you're closed for a personal matter."

"Except for those looking for a hot beverage."

She giggled and nodded. "Except for them. And Cresswell-on-Wyrd is not like most British villages, in that our shops actually open on Sundays for the same reason: friends and neighbors also realized some customers can only get to the shops on Sundays."

As we settled into the front alcove, I pointed out the window.

"That's where I hope the sandwich board sign will help. If it's out, then I'm open."

"Then I suppose I better take it in when I turn the sign to closed."

Walking over to the door, I lifted the open/closed sign off the nail before plucking the nail from the door. Tilda gasped as she watched me walk behind the counter. With a flourish, I ceremoniously tossed the sign and the nail in the garbage.

"There. One problem solved."

Before returning to the alcove, I picked up a tray and filled it with cups and saucers as well as the carafe of cinnamon-cardamom tea. It was too late in the day for caffeine, but I wanted a hot beverage to soothe my frayed nerves. It would relax me while I filled Tilda in on my strained interaction with Lewis.

12

Tilda and I chatted quietly about nothing in particular, suddenly hesitant as we both were to address more serious topics. Juggling everything in my head was wearing on me, and I suspected Tilda didn't want to cause me any more anxiety. But I knew we had to get moving on updating herbal formulations for Cinnamon and multiple humans as well. It was time to forge ahead, so I took a sip of my tea and placed it unceremoniously on the table.

"I feel like there are a few elephants in this room that we're both skirting."

This time, Tilda's giggle was less effusive, more nervous.

"My, aren't you the intuitive one today. Yes, I would agree with you."

"Now that we've gotten that awkwardness out of the way, where shall we start?"

"Where indeed? What would you like to address, Rowan?"

I stared up at the ceiling as I tapped my index finger against my lips.

"Based on this morning's revelation by Elspeth, I'm thinking about '*some spices are better left unspoken'*."

"Oh? I thought we had put that one to bed. Both Cinnamon and I recall Betty using that particular expression, ad nauseam really, around catmint."

"True. But..."

Frustrated that Tilda wasn't connecting the dots, I held my words for a few seconds. I could almost see the gears switching in her brain, as it dawned on her that I was referring to yet another spice.

"Clove! You think Betty meant it for clove too."

Finally! Thankful that her voice sounded inquisitive instead of accusatory, I pressed on.

"That's exactly what I'm thinking. I've been reviewing some of Betty's earlier entries in her Steep Secrets."

"And what did you discover?"

"Well, she included some medical information about the spice: that clove aids in digestion and inflammation. People like to add it to various food and drink for warmth, spice, and depth. She also wrote that it acts as a natural preservative and can extend the shelf life of foods."

"All interesting and all true. But what does that have to do with it being left unspoken?"

A sound beyond the couch startled us both. One of the pups—I couldn't tell if it was Pudding or Pickles—was chasing a squirrel in their dream. The furious feet kicking away made contact with their sibling, who yipped and rolled away. We chuckled as quietly as we could, so as not to wake them. I was hoping they'd stay sleeping until it was time to close up for the day and return them to my father at the pub and inn. Tilda motioned towards the kitchen as she picked up our used teacups. Nodding, I followed behind her, pausing to return the carafe of cinnamon-cardamom tea to the counter. Tilda continued the conversation from the sink.

"We can speak at length in here without waking those lovelies. And we'll hear the bell if anyone pops in."

I sat at the table, encouraging her to join me instead of doing the washing up. Shrugging, she dried off her hands and sat across from me.

"All I was thinking about Betty's innocuous entry was that she was covering for something else. In my mind, it makes total sense that she would write out something so nondescript for an herb she wanted to stay away from."

"And you're basing that assessment on…what?"

"Well, from everything I've learned about her since arriving in the village: between what people have said, what they haven't said, what I've read in her books, what we've discussed."

My words were having an impact on Tilda. She appeared to be accepting of my analysis.

"I have no reason to doubt your judgment here, Rowan. Betty was gifted; her intuition was even stronger than mine. Being related to her, I'm certain you have that gift too."

I wasn't so sure about that, but I let it go. There were definitely strange connections between me and other residents of Cresswell-on-Wyrd, but I wouldn't necessarily characterize it as a gift.

"These comments were written in her very early notes, before she had begun to create her cryptic code. That's why I think it's another type of code."

"Okay, I'll buy it. Let's put this one to bed, then. What else would you like to discuss and/or solve? You're such a great sleuth, I'm sure you've been analyzing everything."

Chuckling before I responded, I reflected on what I'd been thinking about lately.

"More like over-analyzing, if I'm being honest. I think you're right to add Lewis to my list of suspects for the anonymous note. My question is, how did it manage to be delivered with the mail when it didn't have any postage?"

Tilda banged both hands on the table as she rose out of her seat. Her expression was part lightbulb going off above her head, part annoyance at her latest brain wave.

"Delivered with the mail, you say?"

Nodding at her question, I waited for her to continue. She snapped her fingers as she laughed.

"I bet I know exactly how that went down, as you youngsters like to say."

Tilda's expression made me groan, but not as much as her referring to me as a youngster.

"Do tell."

"If we think the note sender was one of the Smeaton lads and/or Lewis, it's plain as day to me."

"Not to me. Please explain."

"Our friendly, neighborhood mail carrier."

"You mean Stan?"

"The one and only Stan Pigeon. The man is lonely, and he's always inviting the young lads to join him for a pint. Lewis being the unscrupulous schemer that we know and don't love, I could see him cajoling Stan into delivering it for them."

"You mean, in exchange for a coveted pint together? That's definitely a theory. And I wouldn't put it past Lewis. I suppose that would push him to the top of my list."

"And I wouldn't discount Chase and Hunter's role in a scheme like that. Stan wants to be friends with all three of them. You never know if they conspired to get Stan to do their bidding."

"That's the second reference to conspiracies this week.

Last week, we were talking about curses with that darned catmint. Now, we're talking about conspiracies."

Tilda giggled and rubbed her hands together, looking remarkably like an evil genius in the process.

"Yes, it's all very cloak and dagger, wouldn't you agree? The cursed catmint, the clove conspiracy. So much intrigue for our boring little village."

I laughed at her assessment. "Personally, I wouldn't say there was anything boring about this village. It's been one crazy adventure after another since I arrived."

"Yes, you've had your fair share of exploits in Cresswell-on-Wyrd."

"Honestly, I was hoping things would quiet down this week. Then my dad arrived, so I know the next little while will be anything but quiet."

No sooner had I uttered the word quiet than we heard a commotion erupting in the front of the shop. We rose as one and raced through the swinging doors. Cinnamon was standing in the middle of the shop, hissing and turning from side to side. Pudding and Pickles were running around him, barking joyously. Their tiny curlicue tails were flying in all directions, in the pug version of a wag.

With eerie precision, the two dogs stopped circling and rubbed up against the distressed cat. From our vantage point, it looked like the pugs were fawning over him. Cinnamon appeared disgusted at the physical contact. For a fleeting moment, I could have sworn I saw a smile creep across his whiskered face. This moment called for some cat chat, so I went to the counter to retrieve my go-to cardamom blend. Placing it on the floor in front of Cinnamon, I was surprised to see both Pudding and Pickles jockey to shove their snouts in the opening. Cinnamon sat back on his haunches and exhaled loudly. Having smelled enough of the blend when I first brought it over, Cinnamon began speaking.

"I thought I told you I don't share. Particularly not with...mutts."

He spit out the last word, turning his back on the pugs. They joined in the conversation, much to everyone's surprise.

"Well, get used to it, kitty cat. That's the way the cookie crumbles. Bob's your uncle, and all that. The name's Pickles, not mutt."

Not to be outdone, Pudding jumped into the conversation. "Au contraire, mon frère. You are using that British saying incorrectly."

"Philistines." The last word emerged from Cinnamon's mouth before he stalked off to his cat bed in the kitchen.

Me, I was flabbergasted by this sudden turn of events. Tilda, on the other hand, was giggling uncontrollably and clapping her hands together.

"What a delightful development! Three-way cross-species communication. Betty would have been so thrilled."

"There's that, sure. But how are we going to keep it quiet. These two aren't exactly shrinking violets. At least Cinnamon is more or less content to be contained in the shop."

Tilda stopped what she was doing and looked me in the eye. The change in her demeanor was not lost on me. She too understood the challenge we were facing. Suddenly, she snapped her fingers and broke into a smile.

"I've got it! We still have their carrier here. I'll pile them in, cover it with a blanket and secret them to your father across the road."

She leaned towards me to whisper the next part, so I obliged her and leaned forward too. "I'll tell them we want it to be a surprise for Reginald, so they have to stay quiet until I remove the blanket in a flourish." Tilda waved her arm in the air, mimicking the movement she was describing. It was a bit half-brained, but I didn't have any other ideas. I nodded in agreement. It would have to do for now.

"Okay, that would be great, Tilda. While you do that, I'll close up the shop and meet the two of you in the pub for dinner. Give me about half an hour to get sorted."

Not wasting a moment, Tilda leaned over and scratched Pudding—or Pickles, I still couldn't tell them apart—on the top of their head. It brought both of them back to the moment, and they sat down at Tilda's feet.

"Listen, my lovelies. We need to surprise Reginald with your new ability. Are you game?"

Excited barking was interspersed with words, in both English and French.

"Arf, splendid idea, arf."

"Oui, oui, woof. Let's do le surprise."

Tilda led the pugs toward the front door and their awaiting carrier. I followed behind with the blanket they had been sleeping on. After they left, I leaned against the door in relief. Talking dogs was not on my bingo card that morning. It was a hilarious complication that I'd need to unravel, along with my growing list of mysteries.

13

Cinnamon stayed far away from the shop as I cleaned up. When I carried the carafes into the kitchen, he made a point of turning his back on me in a huff.

"Still smarting from your new friends' ability to speak?"

He harrumphed before responding. "If you must know, I don't relish sharing my precious space with dirty hounds."

"Aren't you the melodramatic one? They're not staying with us. I secured the one and only room at the inn. They'll be staying across the road with my father."

This last statement drew him out of his cat bed. Walking towards me, he jumped on the table so he could be closer to my eye level. Fixing me with a steely gaze, he appeared to be speaking through gritted teeth and pursed lips.

"Be that as it may, you and I both know they'll be in the shop during the day. Which means I will not."

"Alrighty then! Have it your way. You're more than welcome to stay upstairs in the suite when they're here."

"I can and I shall."

I turned away from the table and continued to the sink.

Placing the carafes down one by one, I opened each lid and poured the remaining contents down the drain.

"Do what you've got to do. But I think you're missing an opportunity here. If you don't want to continue our experiments to find a more permanent solution for your speaking, Tilda and I can always shift our efforts to the pugs."

As I had hoped, this got under Cinnamon's skin. I suspected he was feeling less 'special' now that we had discovered other animals' speech could be unlocked with herbal blends. Not wanting to hurt his feelings, especially after the revelation about his time as a kitten, I turned around to face him. Softening my voice, I walked over and scratched his favorite spot between his eyes.

"I'm sorry, Cinnamon. This must be a lot for you. When my dad comes over tomorrow with Pudding and Pickles, you take as much time as you need upstairs."

My gesture and words seemed to have a calming effect on his demeanor. He rubbed up into my hand, purring first before speaking.

"*Fine*. You're forgiven. This time."

Cinnamon was still a fickle feline, and his last statement caused me to chuckle. I gave him a pat on the head before heading back into the shop. With everything that had happened this week, I wanted to be doubly certain I had locked the front door. As I emerged from the kitchen, I remembered that the sandwich board was still set up on the sidewalk out front. When I got closer, I could see an unfamiliar man glancing nervously at the board.

Scruffy was a polite way to refer to his appearance. Although worn, his clothing appeared well made, likely having cost a pretty penny. His hair was long and unkempt, as was his beard. Holes in his backpack risked the contents escaping. His trousers were worn with dried mud caked along the bottoms. Still, his presence in front of Black Thumb Betty's did not frighten me in the least. Opening the door slowly—I didn't want to startle him—I smiled and greeted him like any other customer.

"Hello. I'm just closing up for the day, but I could brew you a tea or coffee to take away."

My presence in the doorway did in fact catch him off guard. When he heard my voice, he jumped back a bit and looked like he was about to run.

"It's okay. You don't need to come in if you'd prefer to stay outside. Just tell me what you'd like, and I'll pop into the back to prepare it for you."

Still not speaking, he pointed at the sandwich board. It still read:

Sweater (jumper) found. Please inquire within.

Was this the mystery person from the tunnel?

"Are you here about the sweater? Um, I mean jumper."

His voice cracked as he finally spoke. It sounded like he hadn't spoken in a few days and was likely dehydrated too.

"Y-y-y-yes. My jumper, please."

"Would you like to come in while I fetch it? I have cold water too, if you'd like something other than a hot beverage."

Nodding, he walked towards me as I held the door open for him. I pointed towards the couch in the front alcove, inviting him to sit down. He glanced down at his less-than-immaculate clothes by way of explanation.

"Don't worry about a little dirt. A cat and two dogs have been sleeping on it as of late. If anything, you'll be dirtier and the couch will be cleaner afterwards."

I laughed nervously, hoping he'd appreciate my attempt

at levity. It seemed to have worked, as he smiled shyly and walked towards the couch. Before retrieving his sweater, I picked up the water pitcher and two glasses from the counter, placing them on the table in front of him. He obliged me by filling both glasses, though his was emptied in seconds flat when it reached his lips. I nodded to encourage him to refill it and drink more.

When I returned to the table with his sweater, the pitcher of water was empty. The stranger was eyeing my full glass, so I pushed it towards him. He mumbled thanks and inhaled the water in what felt like one rather long sip. The empty glass bounced as he dropped it on the table, rolling towards the edge. We both laughed and any tension in the room was lifted. I held up the sweater.

"I believe this belongs to you."

He snatched it from my hands and hugged it to his chest. The brashness of his action caught me off guard, but I wasn't worried for my safety. It felt more like the sweater had great sentimental value to him and he was relieved to have it back.

"I'm sorry if I seem rude. It's been a challenging few days. And I thought I had lost this. My wife knit this for me before she died. It still smells like her," he lifted it to his nose as he spoke, inhaling deeply.

"That must have been overwhelming when you thought it was gone. I'm happy that I was able to help reunite you with it..."

I looked at him questioningly, hoping he would share his name with me.

"The name's Bramble, Peter Bramble."

"Nice to meet you, Peter. I'm Rowan Thorne and this is the shop I inherited from my dead Aunt Betty. Hence the name, Black Thumb Betty's."

"Thank you so much for saving my jumper, um, I guess you say sweater, Rowan. It means the world to me."

Now that we were on a first-name basis, I felt it was appropriate to inquire about where I had found the sweater.

"My pleasure. I understand completely. My mother passed away a few years ago, and I still hang on to one of her favorite scarves."

I smiled a melancholy smile, hoping to foster a mutual sense of love and loss. He murmured his apologies, visibly more relaxed than when he had first entered the shop.

"Peter, might I ask you about where I found your sweater?"

He laughed nervously and leaned back on the couch. I hoped my directness wouldn't shut down his sharing.

"You mean the tunnel?"

"The tunnel, yes. What exactly were you doing down there?"

"Well, you see I'm a rambler and a volunteer with the National Rambling Association."

"Yes, I've heard of ramblers. I know many Brits enjoy the walking path that cuts through Cresswell-on-Wyrd parallel to Sycamore Row."

Peter seemed excited that I had heard of the NRA, much different than the American organization that bore the same abbreviation.

"That's right. I had volunteered to maintain the walking paths in this part of Gloucestershire. Since I hadn't been to the area before, I was keen to explore a new place. No sad memories of Stella—that was my wife's name—on these walking paths."

"Fresh start, I get that. It's why you're chatting with an American. I needed a fresh start too."

"Quite. Well, I'm not familiar with the area, so I got

caught along your garden path after dark. I lost my wallet, so I couldn't pay for accommodations and it was too dark to walk the 12 miles to the next village, where I had parked my car."

"Oh dear, that must have been stressful for you."

"Stressful, yes. But I was also kicking myself for poor planning. You see, Stella used to make all the plans when we would go rambling. I didn't bring a backup torch, I mean flashlight, or spare batteries either. When I walked around the bushes to look for somewhere to lay my head, I discovered the entrance to the tunnel. It seemed a safer—and drier—place to rest until the sun came."

"We heard you down there. Why were you scratching at a sealed door?"

I pointed towards the now-sealed secret entrance to the tunnel, hidden once again behind a bookcase.

"We?"

"My cat Cinnamon and me. He ran over and started sniffing around the entrance. Thank goodness he did because I thought I was hallucinating when I first heard you."

"I apologize profusely. My torch had burnt out, and I got turned around in the pitch black. I thought I had climbed the other staircase and couldn't figure out how to open it up. Then I remembered that I had opened a hatch to descend the stairs, so I realized there must be a second staircase in play."

I pretended to wipe sweat off my brow as I laughed.

"Phew! That's such a relief. For a moment, I thought someone was after me."

"Oh dear, Rowan. Again, my sincerest apologies for causing you such distress."

"Well, now that that's resolved, I can cross you off my list."

"List? That sounds ominous. Why do you have a list?"

"Long story, I won't bore you. Suffice it to say, not everyone likes my presence here. And I'm still trying to figure out why that is."

"I'm relieved I'm not on your list. Does anyone else know about this list?"

"Just my friend Tilda. You may have seen her leave with a pet carrier shortly before we met."

Shaking his head, Peter looked agitated once again. He jumped up from the couch, making a beeline for the door.

"Oh no! This is not good, not good at all."

I quickly followed, trying to ascertain his concern.

"What's wrong with Tilda knowing about you?"

"The NRA has a very strict code of conduct. Under no circumstances are volunteers to breach private property. If they find out I slept in the tunnels, they'll banish me for life!"

"Slow your roll, Peter. Tilda is one of the most trustworthy people I've ever met. I'll let her know this is a zip-the-lips scenario. You have my word."

"That's such a relief, Rowan. Rambling was our shared hobby. I feel like Stella is walking with me when I'm on the paths."

Peter was asking me to keep a secret—yet another secret swirling around in my brain. The only saving grace was that this one would be shared with Tilda. This definitely felt to me like a burden shared is a burden halved, but it was still a secret. I sighed, knowing I would keep Peter's confidence, no matter how hard it was.

"You have my word, Peter. We'll keep your presence in the tunnel under wraps."

As we stood at the doorway, it dawned on me that the sun had set. Had Peter been wandering around the village, looking for his sweater? He was about to leave when I grabbed his arm.

"Hang on a minute. Where are you sleeping tonight?"

My question caught him off guard. His eyes darted to and fro, without making eye contact with me.

"Well..."

"Were you planning to sleep in the tunnel again?"

"Needs must, I suppose."

"That's no good. We can't risk someone else spotting you there. Not to mention how cold and dark it is down there."

He held up his hands in mock surrender.

"I'm out of options, though. My car is 12 miles away, I lost my wallet, and the only room to let in this village is occupied."

"By my father, actually. He just arrived from America for an extended visit."

"So, I can't expect him to vacate the room at the inn for me."

"No, unfortunately. But I might have an idea."

I motioned back into the shop before continuing. "Why don't you take a seat on the couch and I'll be back shortly."

With that, I dashed out the door. Running across Sycamore Row, I was thankful for the quiet evening. I hadn't even checked for bicycles or cars before I leapt off the sidewalk.

14

The lights were still on in Wyrd's Remedies & Chemist. Gideon too was doing his closing routine. I took a deep breath before knocking on the door. There was no love lost between us, and our most recent encounter had left me unsettled. But I was hopeful he would see that my request could potentially benefit him as well.

When he heard my knock, Gideon looked up as he tapped his watch with his index finger. When he saw it was me, he scrunched up his face in dismay. I suspected my appearance had raised his blood pressure. Holding up all the fingers on one hand to indicate I needed five minutes of his time, I crossed the fingers of my other hand behind my back. Was my idea a little bit nutsy coo coo? Most definitely. Would he be willing? Only time would tell.

Gideon took his sweet time walking to the door and unlocking. It felt like he had already started the five-minute timer and was trying to run it out before even hearing me out.

"Sorry to disturb, Gideon. I have a wild request, but I'm hoping you'll listen to it all before making a decision."

He rolled his eyes but still held the door open for me to enter.

"I'll give you four minutes. This better be good."

I explained about Peter's presence in my shop—without sharing details on his night in the tunnel.

"My father is occupying the only room at the Hare & Harrow. I know you wanted to convert Tilda's old suite into a short-term rental."

Gideon started shaking at my last comment, still smarting from the Village Council's ban on his plan to earn extra income. He looked like he would start spitting nails if he spoke. I held up my hand and tried to soften my gaze.

"Please, let me finish before you kick me out. What I'm proposing is you let Peter stay the night in your suite. I'm sure Peter will provide a glowing reference, and I'll put in a good word for you. I'd be happy to speak on your behalf at the next Village Council meeting. It really is inconvenient to only have one room to let in the entire village."

My words had a calming effect on the pharmacist. The color in his face returned to his normal pale pall. He seemed to be breathing normally again. The man who had previously wanted me to leave the village picked me up in a bone-crushing hug and spun us both around.

"Rowan, you're brilliant! Yes, yes, please invite Mr. Peter Bramble over right away. He can stay as many days as he needs to."

I laughed at Gideon's sudden exuberance, relieved he liked my idea. Tilda's removal of Gideon from my list of suspects made total sense to me now. He wasn't trying to drive me out of the village. He was just a concerned family man trying to protect his family. I hoped this latest development would heal the fractures between us.

"That's fantastic, Gideon. Thank you! Let me run back to my shop and fetch Peter. Please don't be surprised by his unkempt nature, he's mourning his wife, and I don't think he's gotten back into a regular routine of self-care."

"Of course, of course. I won't mention his appearance."

I was back with Peter in a matter of minutes. He was feeling shy about entering another shop in his state, but his reticence disappeared when he saw Gideon standing at the door. His arms were open in welcome and his smile lit up his entire face. It was the most pleasant I had seen him since moving to COW.

"Come in, come in. Peter Bramble, it's lovely to meet you. As I was telling Rowan, you can stay one night or multiple nights. The suite is set up for short-term rentals, and you will be my first guest."

Peter smiled and wiped a tear from the corner of his eye. He was genuinely pleased and kept shaking Gideon's hand in thanks. Gideon grabbed him by the shoulders and turned him from side to side.

"Is, is everything alright, sir?"

"Please, no sir here. Sir was my father. Call me Gideon. Your trousers are a little worse for wear. I believe we're close to the same size, and I have a spare pair of trousers in the back room. They may be a little short for you, but they should still fit. Shall I fetch them for you before we head upstairs?"

Peter choked up at Gideon's warmth and generosity. Frankly, I too was surprised to see this side of him. Maybe I had indeed misread him all along. I waved to both and headed back to my own shop, stopping midstride in the middle of the road. My father and Tilda were still waiting for me in the pub, and I had been much longer than the 30 minutes I had initially indicated. I turned once again and passed the window of Gideon's shop on my way to the pub. There was no reason to keep them waiting any longer, my shop could stay unlocked for an hour or so.

15

Entering the Hare & Harrow from the dark road caused me to pause. My eyes needed a moment to adjust to the lights. But my ears were working perfectly fine. What I heard was my father's snorting laugh and Tilda's tinkling giggle. They sounded like they were old friends. The fact that the two most important people in my life were getting along so well warmed my heart. I had been slightly apprehensive about my father's visit, but it appeared I had no reason to be.

Walking past the bar, I ignored the sneering face Lewis was making at me. He was definitely still on the top of my list of suspects. His grandmother, Moira, my fellow member of the Catmint Council, stood at the other end of the bar. She nodded towards me then proceeded to scold her adult grandson. He was pouring the draft incorrectly, resulting in too much foam.

His sneer turned to frustration, and I watched his ears turn a bright red. I wondered briefly if Moira's display was for my benefit. Glancing at Moira, I saw her wink at me before turning away. Someone else in my corner, I was relieved to see. As I approached my father and Tilda, she let out a breathy laugh. It sounded as if she was deflating. I smiled at the both of them and looked under the table before sitting down.

"Where are the pugs?"

"Oh, Rowan. You should have seen those two scallywags. They were so excited to see your father, they wore themselves out jumping and spinning. We left a pile of pugs snoozing at the foot of the bed."

I glanced around as I sat down, making sure no one was in direct ear shot. Still, I felt the need to whisper my questions.

"Did they? Were they?"

My father leaned forward and continued the whisper game.

"Speaking? Is that what you want to know?"

"Pretty much, yup."

"They were. And it was glorious. Pudding told me she loved me. And Pickles said they understand everything I say to them."

"Wow, that's huge! It's taken me so long to get Cinnamon to trust me and share. Even now, he's still as stubborn as the day is long."

My father leaned back and let loose with the biggest snorting laugh yet. His movement made me think once again of Piper. Was it really a British mannerism, or was there more there? Did I want to dive down this rabbit hole, no matter the cost? I shuddered at the thought but knew it wasn't the time to delve. I'd put a pin in it for now, but my father and I needed to have a frank discussion next time we were alone. My gut was telling me there was something there. As much as I didn't want to admit Tilda's woo woo view of my intuition, I had to acknowledge that she might be right in this instance.

"To be fair, the pugs have been in my life for a few years now. We had already developed a bond of trust. Cinnamon has only known you for a New York minute. You need to give him time to build that bond with you."

Tilda jumped into our conversation. "And he is a cat, after all. They play by their own rules. Dogs, though, there's a reason they're called man's best friend."

"Okay, you're both right, I suppose. And I'll have some fences to mend with Cinnamon tonight. He was not pleased about Pudding and Pickles when they started talking. And then when he discovered them in his bed, well..."

Tilda reached across the table and patted my hand reassuringly. "His ego is wounded. For years, he's been a party of one. I'm sure a part of him believed the herbs worked on him and him alone. His entire identity has just been shattered."

"You make a good point. I never thought of it that way."

Our conversation was halted by Moira's appearance. She was carrying a tray of drinks, menus tucked under her arm. After setting the drinks on the table, she tossed the menus down and wedged the tray under her arm.

"I hear we may need another council meeting."

"Village Council? Why?"

Tsk-ing as she shook her head, Moira was clearly disappointed that I hadn't picked up on her meaning.

"Not Village Council," she leaned forward and muttered through pursed lips, "Catmint Council. More animal behavior that needs to be addressed."

Tilda turned to survey the room. Satisfied that no one was in ear shot, she picked up on Moira's message.

"Agreed. The dogs were, ahem, not as quiet as I had hoped when I arrived with them."

"Now that's the understatement of the year, Tilda. They were shouting 'Squirrel! Écureuil! SQUIRREL!' as you barreled through the door. Luckily, the pub was quiet, with no customers in sight and the staff were assembled in the kitchen for a meeting. We were able to get them up to your father before anyone heard them."

The cross-language mix was alive and well with the pugs. They had still been speaking both English and French after they left Black Thumb Betty's. I was equal parts concerned and excited at this revelation. Their exuberance meant they didn't know how to be discreet. Or want to, for that matter.

It was just how Cinnamon had acted when he got hold of the triple c cocoa (with a kick), full of cinnamon, cardamom, and cayenne. In that case, he had spoken English as well as barking like a dog at my reopening event, Cuppa Comeback. And the failed experiment with Sleep Salve and that cursed catmint, which had caused him to publicly sing show tunes from the musical *Cats*. In both cases, I had been able to cover for him, with no undue consequences.

The pugs, though, seemed to be loose cannons. We would definitely have to keep them away from herbal blends in the shop and elsewhere. My attention was brought back to the present when I felt a tug on my sleeve.

It was my father, who appeared to be leaving our little gathering. "I'll head up to my room until your meeting adjourns."

His comment confused me. Perplexed, I looked at Tilda and Moira in turn.

"Meeting? What meeting?"

Moira was still frustrated with me, and it showed in her response.

"The *Council.* I just told you we need a meeting of the Catmint Council."

"Oh, you mean now? That wasn't clear at all."

Tilda sprang up from her seat when she saw Arthur hobble through the pub entrance. Right behind him was Reverend Basil Primrose, looking quite hot under the collar. The Reverend towered over Arthur, and he shot a nod of greeting to the equally tall Moira as he entered. Moira turned towards the bar and hollered at her grandson.

"Lewis, tend the bar. We're have a meeting of the Tea Preservation Society."

TPS, or Tea Preservation Society, was the cover for the Catmint Council. Publicly, the TPS boasted that their focus was to ensure that English Breakfast tea remained the official tea of the British Isles. Privately, it had become the Catmint Council, as the secretive society worked to keep Cinnamon's speaking abilities just that—a secret from the villagers and outsiders alike. Judging from the demeanor of those in attendance, I was worried they might shut down my work to help Cinnamon communicate on a more regular basis.

The five of us—me, Tilda, Moira, Arthur, and Basil—sat shoulder to shoulder around the small, circular table. It had been chosen because of its distance from the bar and other patrons. No one would be able to overhear our conversation unless they sat down at one of the tables in this darkest corner of the pub. We ignored the fact that our knees were touching under the table, focusing instead on the crucial conversation that needed to happen. The Reverend opened the meeting, opting to whisper even though we were not in anyone's ear shot.

"Moira, we'll dispense with meeting minutes for the time being. I trust your stellar photographic memory will do us justice when you record them later this evening. Preferably, when you are alone."

Moira nodded curtly, seemingly annoyed that Reverend Primrose questioned her discretion with his comments. I was momentarily distracted when a hand brushed my knee. Tilda tried to stifle a giggle, and Arthur's blush turned his face and neck a deep crimson. His hand was clearly meant for Tilda's knee, not mine. Both Primrose and Moira glared at the schoolyard antics of the lovebirds. I couldn't say I blamed them, but I was also happy that my friends had found love. Reverend Primrose pressed on, undaunted by the interruption.

"Rowan, you need to explain yourself. What possessed you to feed secret herbal blends to two unknown entities?"

The directness of the Reverend's question, coupled with his accusatory tone, got my hackles up. Instead of asking for a summary of the events leading up to the dogs talking, he was assuming I had been complicit in the act. Given our history of secretly working together to cure his insomnia, I felt particularly hurt that he would behave so aggressively towards me. Fight fire with fire, I thought.

"Unknown entities? They're dogs, not entities. And if you must know..." he interrupted me before I could finish my thought.

"I must and I shall."

Not wanting to inflame the situation anymore, I bit my tongue before continuing. A few deep breaths were in order, to calm my temper and even out my voice.

"If you must know," I began again, more calmly this time, "it was a complete accident. Pudding and Pickles ran up to Cinnamon as he was sniffing the speaking blend. To be honest, I was as surprised as the rest of you that the pugs were able to speak."

Another giggle from Tilda distracted the lot of us. Reverend Primrose turned towards her, ready to let loose with a few choice words. This budding romance between Tilda and Arthur was interfering with Council business. Personally, I wondered if it would impact the power dynamics of the Catmint Council.

Arthur jumped in before Primrose could chastise Tilda "Apologies, Basil. I was just sharing a private joke with Tilda. Didn't intend to disrupt the meeting."

"Arthur, need I remind you that there are no private issues at Council meetings, jokes or otherwise. If it was important enough to interrupt the flow of the meeting... well, go on then, let's hear it."

At my first meeting with this group, Reverend Primrose had made me feel like a school-aged child being sent to the principal's office. Now he was trying to act the same way towards a man who was most definitely his senior. Arthur was having none of it, though.

"Enough already, Basil. You are not the headmaster, and this is not school."

I hazarded glances at the other women around the table. We were all trying to keep straight faces, even though this moment warranted a good hearty laugh. Once we made eye contact, all bets were off. Guffaws and giggles circulated the table, with Arthur joining in. After what seemed like an interminably long time, but was probably only a dozen or so seconds, the Reverend too relaxed and grudgingly joined in the laughter. The tension broken, we got back to the business at hand. I jumped in to refocus the conversation.

"Look, there's an easy solution to all of this."

"Go on," the Reverend had gotten off his high horse and seemed genuinely interested in what I had to say.

"I opened the jar with the speaking spice blend on the floor, which is how the pups were able to access it. If we keep it contained and away from them, it won't happen again."

Tilda was bursting at the seams, waiting for me to finish my thought so she could jump in. She seemed so excited she was practically tipping off her chair.

"Hang on, Rowan. While I agree that we shouldn't allow the darlings to access the herbs unsupervised, I feel we'd be missing a wonderful research opportunity if we followed your suggestion."

Her comment intrigued everyone gathered, and murmurs were heard as I replied. "What are you thinking, Tilda?"

"For the longest time, Betty believed that Cinnamon was unique. A one-of-a-kind animal who possessed special abilities that she was learning to unlock. Perhaps, though, it's something to do with our magical village *combined* with special herbal blends."

"Why did you say the village is magical? Is there something you're not telling us?" I was surprised that my tone sounded somewhat accusatory, but Tilda took no offence and smiled before replying.

"Ah yes, apologies for my vagueness. One time, Betty travelled with Cinnamon. She had taken supplies with her so Cinnamon would be able to communicate. But about an hour outside the village, the herbal blends were useless to her. Cinnamon could only meow, growl, hiss, and purr."

This revelation was shocking, to say the least. A frisson of excitement rippled through the air.

"Tilda, is this why you're always going on about my intuition and other 'woo woo' links in the village?"

She giggled when I said 'woo woo' but nodded her head nonetheless.

"Precisely. Betty and I discussed it, and we believed that there are magical elements in Cresswell-on-Wyrd and the surrounding area that contribute to Cinnamon's ability to speak."

Arthur looked surprised at Tilda's confession. Checking on Moira and Reverend Primrose, I was astonished to see that they were not taken aback by Tilda's comments. I looked at them questioningly until Moira spoke up.

"Well, there have been rumors circulating for hundreds of years that Cresswell-on-Wyrd is a magical destination, at the convergence of multiple ley lines."

This conversation was becoming more baffling to me, not less. "I'm sorry, ley lines? I've never even heard of them."

"You wouldn't have, Rowan, as Americans are not as attuned to the earth as we Brits are. No offence intended, just stating facts."

I shook my head at Moira's apology. "None taken. So, what are ley lines?"

"Ley lines have to do with the earth's energy and magnetic field. In a nutshell, they're believed to connect mystical sites around the world."

"You mean, like Stonehenge?"

Moira gave a curt nod and continued. "Precisely. These areas of altered magnetic fields, around invisible ley lines, seem to draw animals to them."

Tilda jumped in to help Moira with the explanation. "There is also great speculation that they can cause nausea and headaches. Betty was focused on herbal teas that addressed these types of complaints, which is why she eschewed black tea in favor of the medicinal benefits in many herbs."

The Reverend nodded at Tilda's comments, adding his own spin on the discussion. "While I still stand behind the work of the Tea Preservation Society, I do support the work Betty was doing with her herbal blends. The side effects from living near ley lines can be nasty."

My head was spinning from all this new information. And we still hadn't resolved the issue of the pugs' ability to speak. I was hungry and I suspected my father was ready to gnaw off his arm. Not wanting to keep him waiting in his room any longer, I held up my hands in a T formation to indicate I wanted a time out.

"This is a lot of new information to absorb. Can we pause this meeting and resume it at another day and time? My father is waiting to dine with me, and I'm so hungry I could eat a horse. If any of you would like to join us, you're more than welcome to."

Reverend Primrose stood and began to move away from the table. "Rowan makes a good point. We shall resume this meeting tomorrow evening, at the church. I will take my leave and sup at the vicarage. Good evening to you all."

He turned as he reached the pub entrance. His final words to us were spoken as he was halfway out the door, causing me to suspect his food was growing cold at home.

"Oh, and meeting adjourned."

16

Moira rose from the table and returned to the bar. I knew she didn't entirely trust her grandson to hold down the fort, even when she was only 10 feet away. Arthur and Tilda settled into the table, leaning against each other. Judging from their posture, they would be joining my father and I for dinner. I jumped up and headed to the stairs that led to the only room at the inn.

Knocking on the door, I heard my father trying to quiet the pugs. They seemed excited at the prospect of visitors. My father opened the door a crack, his foot in the opening to block any potential canine escapes.

"Hey Dad. Our meeting is over. Are you ready to eat? Arthur and Tilda will be joining us."

"Right-o, Rowan. These two need a quick walk and nature break before that. Could you order for me, and I'll join you in 20 minutes or so?"

"I have a better idea. I can help you take them for a walk, and we'll ask them to order for both of us."

"Splendid! I would love the company."

My father opened the door wider to allow me entry. I leaned over to shoo the dogs back inside before closing the door behind me. He handed me one leash and pointed to the dog at my feet. The leash was color-coded, and I had no idea which dog used the green leash and which one used the yellow leash.

"Which one is this?" I asked as I attached the leash to the pug's collar.

He was working on corralling the other pup, who didn't seem quite as taken with the prospect of a walk.

"Green is for Pudding. That's Pudding at your feet. She's much better behaved than her brother, as you can see. Pickles, sit! Pickles is a bundle of energy, which is why he has the yellow leash."

"Oh?" The logic was lost on me, so I pressed my father to explain.

"Yellow is supposed to be more soothing than green. That's what the dog trainer I hired told me. Although it doesn't seem to be working right now."

I reached over and plucked the yellow leash from his hand. Using my other hand to scoop up Pickles, I plopped him on the bed. Holding him down while whispering was distraction enough to get the leash attached. My dad snorted out a laugh as I handed him the leash.

"Brilliant, dear. Thank you for your help. This walk is going to go much more smoothly with a second pair of hands."

"Not at all. I'm happy to help. Though I'd like to choose the direction of our walk. We can wander down Smuggler's Lane and back."

"Of course. Any particular reason you're suggesting that route?"

Laughing as I thought of my reason, I realized I was as beholden to a pet as my father was.

"Well, we have to be careful with pets on Sycamore Row. There is a village decree that bars them from the high street. Most of the time, residents look the other way, but I'd rather not run afoul of any temperamental Cresswellians. That, plus I don't want to make Cinnamon jealous by flaunting our walk. Best that we avoid the shop."

"No truer words were spoken. We must keep our four-legged friends content. You lead the way dear."

At the bottom of the stairs, I handed Pudding's leash to my dad so I could give our order to Arthur and Tilda. They waved to us as we exited the pub.

Turning left, it was a quick jog across the road to reach the top of Smuggler's Lane. We took our time, allowing the pugs to sniff all the new smells. They were particularly intrigued by a piece of paper that was crumpled on the ground. Pickles tried to steal it from Pudding, but she stole it right back.

The two of us were laughing so much at their antics, I didn't even notice we weren't alone on the sidewalk. I looked up when I heard someone clearing their throat. It was Percival Smoothe, owner of Secrets & Suds, the village's cleaning supplies shop. Although we hadn't met officially, we both knew of each other. Straightening up, I tapped my dad's wrist to get his attention.

"Hi Percival. This is my father, Reginald Thorne. He and his pups are visiting from America."

Percival looked down his nose at the dogs. His expression revealed his immediate dislike of them. I suspected he wasn't an animal lover in any way, shape, or form. Tilda had mentioned a run-in he and Betty had had shortly before her death. It involved something about Cinnamon trapping him on a table in the shop, hissing at him.

"I don't allow animal wees near my shop. Kindly take them elsewhere to do their business."

With that, he turned on his heel and walked away from us. My father didn't look annoyed, which surprised me given Percival's rude tone. After we saw Percival turn the corner onto Winding Way, my father led Pickles up to the entrance of Secrets & Suds.

"Okay, boy. Time to release the waterworks."

Pickles lifted his leg and got down to business. Not to be left out, Pudding pulled on her leash and joined her brother. When they finished, we turned tail and headed back to the pub as quickly as the pugs' short legs would allow.

I was laughing so hard, I had trouble getting my words out. "That was hilarious and probably the most fun I've had in a while."

My father laughed as he hugged me. "Stick with me kiddo, and you'll be yucking it up every day."

Reginald led the pugs up to his room before joining us in the back of the pub. Our drinks had arrived, and Tilda indicated our food would be ready shortly. Once Reginald sat down with us, we all raised our glasses and toasted Betty.

17

No sooner had our food arrived that I heard a commotion at the bar. Looking up, I saw Lewis arguing with his grandmother, Moira. With an exasperated look on her face, Moira headed towards our table.

"Rowan, I just overheard my obstreperous grandson take a call. A call, I might add, he was not going to pass over to you."

Intrigued, our group had put down their forks in unison as we waited for Moira to continue.

"It seems Cinnamon has busted out of your shop and he's lurking along Sycamore Row."

I was out of my seat and running to the pub door as Moira yelled the rest of the message in my direction.

"Percival called to say he smelled animal urine outside his shop door and was going to report Cinnamon's unauthorized excursion to the RSPCA."

Picking up my pace, I swung open the heavy, oak door so forcefully, it hit the back wall. Cringing at the sound, I turned to apologize to Moira. She waved me on, unconcerned about the state of her door.

Once on Sycamore Row, I looked right and left. Seeing Cinnamon hightailing it towards the Community Hall, I spun to my left and ran after him. Whispering his name, so as not to draw Percival's attention to us, I didn't catch up to the feline until he had turned onto the garden path. He was heading towards the bushes behind Wyrd's Remedies & Chemist, the very bushes that hid the entrance to the secret tunnel.

I reached out to pick up the fleeing cat, who hadn't slowed down one bit even when he made eye contact with me. Suddenly, I felt myself flying through the air. The autumnal forest cover was hiding a tree root which caught up my foot and sent me in a horizontal trajectory. Grabbing Cinnamon, I turned on my side to allow my shoulder to take the weight of both of us as we hit the ground.

My initial reaction was to yell at Cinnamon, but I suppressed any sound when I heard voices on the path. We were fully concealed by the bushes, which had partly broken our fall. Cinnamon knew enough to stay quiet, and we both strained to identify the speakers.

"C'mon, mate. I did my part." The whiny, nasally voice belonged to our mail carrier, Stan Pigeon.

"We won't know if your 'part' was enough until the Great Harvest Bake Off." The response was hissed through clenched teeth, making identification more difficult. And who was 'we'?

"That's not me problem, mate. A deal's a deal. When are we going for that pint? You promised me." For a middle-aged man, Stan was as whiny as a child. In that moment, I could see why the young men in the village avoided him. And his comment clearly reinforced Tilda's suspicions of

Lewis Culpepper or the Smeaton sons being behind the anonymous note.

Or both? It was difficult to tell at this point. I did know that Lewis was tending bar at the Hare & Harrow, but what about Chase and Hunter Smeaton? It could be either one of them talking to Stan right now.

I ducked even further into the brush as I heard footsteps heading my way. The unidentified speaker was walking in this direction, and quickly.

"Like I said when you accosted me on Sycamore Row, we can't be seen together until our little issue is resolved. Don't call us, we'll call you."

And with that, both sets of footsteps retreated. Exhaling quietly through my nose, I slowly counted to 60 before standing up. Placing Cinnamon on the ground, I brushed off my clothing. It seemed a futile endeavor, as many dried bits of leaves clung everywhere. The only solution would be to head home and change.

"Well, Cinnamon, the plot thickens." I patted my jacket pocket, looking for my emergency jar of cardamom pods. It must have fallen out when I took a tumble. There would be no discussion between human and cat until we returned to Black Thumb Betty's. "Let's get you home so we can talk at length."

Cinnamon shook out his long fur, in an attempt to loosen the dried bits of leaves he too had acquired when we hit the ground. His efforts were unsuccessful, so I picked him up and began gently pulling some of the leaves loose. As I retraced our steps, I murmured to him, hoping his earlier disgust at the pugs speaking was now forgotten.

Once on Sycamore Row, I decided to quickly pop into the pub and make my excuses for missing the rest of our meal. Moira had anticipated my early departure, handing me a takeaway bag as I said my goodbyes. My father and Tilda both agreed to continue our respective conversations in the morning.

I hustled Cinnamon into the shop, locking the door as soon as he jumped out of my arms. It was too risky to sit in the front window and talk, so I followed him into the kitchen. Jumping on the table, Cinnamon pawed at the open jar of cardamom before licking his paw. I helped him by squeezing a few pods between my fingers and holding them near his whiskers. He rubbed up against my fingers and then sat back on his haunches.

"You hurt my ear when you grabbed me and we fell."

"Oh my gosh, Cinnamon, I am so, so sorry. I was worried about you. I promise it won't ever happen again."

"It better not."

I bowed my head in shame before responding. "You have my word. Now, can you please tell me what happened to send you running at such a clip?"

"I was sleeping on the couch when I heard arguing outside the shop. The term 'Black Magic Betty' was bandied about more than once."

"Was it the same men we just heard arguing along the garden path?"

"Yes, it was Stan and another man, but I couldn't tell who it was. They took off towards Lover's Lane, and I made my way outside to follow them."

"Yes, I was running late to meet Tilda and Dad for dinner, so I decided to forego locking up the shop. Although, this time, it seems to have worked in our favor. What happened? When I found you, you were running in the opposite direction to Lover's Lane."

Visibly irritated by my question, Cinnamon jumped off the table and headed for his food bowls. One swat was all it took for me to get off my duff and top them up. After cleaning up the mess he'd made, of course. I busied myself making a pot of cinnamon-cardamom tea while Cinnamon ate his fill. Suitably sated, he hopped back on the table and began grooming himself. I joined him with the steeped tea, a cup for me, and a bowl for him. I was hoping the extra boost of herbs to unlock his tongue would keep him talking. At least until we had unpacked this latest escapade.

Sitting down, I poured tea for both of us. I was bursting at the seams to have Cinnamon continue, but I knew the prudent thing was to keep quiet until he was ready to resume his story. Cinnamon knew he was in control of the moment, and he was relishing it. I watched him wander towards the bowl and lap up a few sips of the tea. Leaning back, he finally started speaking again.

"I was pursuing them down Sycamore Row when they turned back towards me. I didn't have time to open the shop door again, so I started booking it towards the Community Hall."

"I was in the pub, eating dinner with my dad, Tilda, and Arthur." I went on to fill Cinnamon in on Lewis's phone call from Percival and reticence to share the news with me.

"There's no love lost between old Percy and me, and he was out for blood. Kept muttering about 'filthy mutts emptying their bladders.'"

I laughed at this assessment, remembering my father's impish reaction to Percival. Cinnamon chuckled grudgingly when I shared the details with him. Maybe he was softening towards the pugs after all.

"Since we know where Lewis was at that time, I wonder if it was Chase or Hunter."

"May have been. I wished I could have told you what was happening before you tackled me into the bushes."

He was still holding a grudge, I could see. I'd let him have his moment. Instead of speaking up, I wandered over to the cutlery drawer to retrieve a knife and fork. The food Moira had packed up for me was still in the sealed takeaway container. Keeping my mouth full would save me from putting my foot in it. And, hopefully, allow Cinnamon the time he needed to wallow before moving on.

My strategy worked, as he wandered over to smell my steak and kidney pie. I ripped a corner off the box and placed a few morsels on it for Cinnamon. Happy to be sharing my meal, I heard him purr as he chewed. I felt enough time had passed for me to weigh in on our conversation.

"My number one priority tomorrow morning will be to get you set up to be able to speak at will. At your will, that is."

My comment caught his attention, as he stopped chewing and looked up at me.

"How are you going to do that?"

I pushed my food to the side, leaning back in my chair so I could access the drawer in the table. It's where I kept *Betty's Steep Secrets*, as well as my own notebook and various lists. Flipping towards the front of Betty's prized recipe book, I stopped when I found the relevant page. It had been folded in half and taped in place. A loose piece of paper was sitting in the home-made pocket, which I pulled out and waved in front of Cinnamon's face.

"I was going through my Aunt Betty's earlier entries, when I came across this."

Cinnamon seemed unimpressed with my waving hand, so I lowered it. I then flipped to another page where I had folded down the corner. The cat was waiting, somewhat impatiently, for me to explain. So I jumped right in.

"This letter is addressed to me from Betty. It says, '*One day, Rowan, you may understand why I named him Cinnamon. It wasn't only because of his coat.*'"

I lowered the letter and instead pointed to the page in *Betty's Steep Secrets* before continuing.

"And here," I slid my finger down the entry, "this is an unfinished entry. Betty described it as a 'slow-release formulation'."

"What of it? I'm not following the jumps you seem to be making in your brain. Spell them out for me. You know, like I'm a *five-year-old child.*"

Oh great, sarcastic Cinnamon was back in the mix. Undaunted, I looked down at the entry, dragging my finger towards the bottom of the page. "Look here, at the bottom." I held the book up to show Cinnamon. He seemed unimpressed and turned away.

"I can speak, but I never said anything about being able to read. Are you mocking me, Rowan?"

"Not at all! Sorry, sorry. All I wanted to point out is that Betty mentions cinnamon in passing in this entry. But she never completed it!"

I clapped my hands together in excitement.

Cinnamon shook his head in frustration. "Again, not seeing the connections in your brain."

"Right, right, right." I reached down and picked up the letter with one hand, pointing to the unfinished entry with the other. "I think...no, *I believe*, that cinnamon is the key to all of this. Betty named you Cinnamon, not just because of the color of your fur, and she wrote about cinnamon in a slow-release formulation."

"So you're saying we need more, not less, cinnamon to help me talk on a regular basis and at my choosing."

"That's exactly what I'm saying! I think it's at least worth testing my theory."

Cinnamon sat pondering my discovery for quite some time. What was he thinking? Now that the possibility of cross-species communication might be unlocked on a more permanent basis, was he having second thoughts? He mumbled something as he jumped off the table, heading to his cat bed. I decided to give him the time and space to process everything that had transpired today. My hope was that the morning would bring a new attitude in him.

After cleaning up the kitchen, I headed to the secret staircase and what I hoped would be a long, uninterrupted sleep. One that was sorely needed after the past few days.

18

Thursday
Two Days Before the Great Harvest Bake Off

Waking up, I reached around me to feel for Cinnamon. He wasn't there, which meant he had fallen asleep in the kitchen. I hoped he would be more open to my potential cinnamon discovery today. I was excited to share my theory with Tilda and discuss it further.

Just as I emerged from the kitchen with the carafes of hot beverages, Tilda arrived at the front of the shop, followed closely by my father. After all the upheaval Cinnamon had endured in the past twenty-four hours, my dad had had the good sense to leave his dogs behind.

I smiled at them both, holding up the carafes to indicate I'd open the door shortly. They smiled back and began an animated discussion that had both of them laughing like schoolchildren. Unlocking the door, I ushered them inside with a brisk fall wind following them in. The breeze was refreshing, but I was still relieved to close the door on it.

Tilda elbowed my father, "Go on, tell her what you said."

My father chuckled wholeheartedly, waving his hand to dismiss Tilda's suggestion. "I'm sure Rowan doesn't want to hear such things."

I walked towards the front alcove to join them, snuggling up to my father like I used to do as a child. He wrapped his arm around my shoulders and pulled me closer.

"Tell me what?"

Tilda jumped in to explain. "He knew Betty longer than me. But we were comparing notes on her, well, idiosyncrasies, I suppose you could say."

"Oh? And what did he say?"

Tilda pulled herself upright in the chair, straightened her shoulders, and cleared her throat. With a very serious expression on her face, she continued. "Reginald lovingly referred to Betty by saying she was one biscuit short of a packet."

No sooner had the last word escaped her lips than both of them were sliding off their seats. They were laughing so hard tears were streaming down their faces. I chuckled along but couldn't bring myself to laugh with the same level of abandon. My mother would have been happy to see my father enjoying himself so much, I thought to myself.

It took them a few minutes to regain their composure. Once they were seated again, I asked if they'd like a hot beverage. With their coffee orders in hand, I rose and headed to the counter. Black coffees all around meant I didn't need a tray to carry everything back to the front alcove. The stackable mugs and carafe made it an easy two-handed job.

Once we were settled back and sipping the liquid gold, I

filled them in on my exploits along the garden path. Tilda agreed with me that it was most probably Chase or Hunter Smeaton who had been arguing with Stan.

"I just don't understand why they want me to leave. If it weren't for Rory and the Blooms, I'd think every person close to my own age was against me!"

A movement out of the corner of my eye caught my attention. At the mention of the Blooms, my father had nervously pulled at his collar. Was his face growing flushed too? Was he still feeling the effects of jet lag and the time change? Or was his visceral reaction directly related to my comment?

My mental list of mysteries to solve was putting this one near the top. After the possible solution for getting Cinnamon to talk and discovering who sent the anonymous note and why, of course. In that moment, everything else that had been occupying my mind seemed to fall away. Surprisingly, that included the stress I was feeling about keeping so many secrets.

"Tilda, I'll need your help with a few things around the shop today. Dad, you're more than welcome to hang out with us, if you'd like. Unless you have other plans."

My father sat upright and looked even more uncomfortable than he had a moment ago. What did the man have up his sleeve?

"Well, I was thinking of doing some sightseeing. Maybe take Pudding and Pickles for a nice long walk along the garden path towards Whiskerleigh."

"That sounds nice! Don't let us keep you. Perhaps you could join us after lunch?"

"That sounds perfect, my dear. Now I should pop over and get the pooches fed before we head out."

He placed a few bills on the table for his coffee, ignoring

my protests. To be honest, I was happy for the extra cash to fill my coffers and thanked him with a kiss on the cheek.

"See you later, Dad."

After my father left the shop, Tilda sprang up from her chair and flopped down beside me on the couch. Her sudden movement sent her into another fit of laughter. Despite her age, she was as giddy as a schoolgirl. Love was definitely in the brisk, fall air.

We had much to discuss and I was debating which topic to broach first. "Would you give me a moment to make a phone call?"

Tilda waved me towards the counter and wall phone. "Of course, do what you need to do. I'll just relax here with another cup of coffee."

I wandered to the phone, picking up the handset and dialing without a second thought. Not quite a month since I'd arrived in this cellphone-free village, and I was already remembering important numbers. Although the Village Council had relaxed their rules on some cell towers in the central business district, I had opted to keep mine tucked away in my suitcase.

"Piper, hi! So sorry for the early call."

Pausing to listen to her response, I laughed at her enthusiastic greeting. "Yes, I figured you'd be prepping in your shop, too. Would Petunia be able to hold down the fort until later this afternoon? I'd love if you could pop over. Okay, great."

Hanging up, I walked back towards the alcove feeling lighter than air. When my father returned, I would put to rest that niggling feeling I'd been having since I first saw the Bloom twins together.

"Why are you grinning like the Cheshire cat? Hmmm?"

Tilda was on to me, but I wasn't yet ready to share my suspicions.

"Me? Oh, it's nothing. I'm just feeling happy to have my dad nearby."

I could sense that I hadn't convinced Tilda, but she knew me better than to press me.

"Fine, you aren't obliged to share. I'll figure it out eventually."

Of that, I was certain, but I wanted this afternoon's "chance encounter" to play out organically. Sitting down next to Tilda, I assumed a more serious tone. We had several crucial mysteries to solve.

"Why do you think that other man told Stan everything hinged on the Great Harvest Bake Off?"

"I've been pondering that very point since you shared last night's exploits with me. I can only surmise that whoever wants you gone is hoping you'll be too distracted to enter any of Black Thumb Betty's specialties in this year's Bake Off."

"Why would that drive me out of the village?"

"Betty was the one who successfully lobbied the Bake Off organizing committee to create a beverage category. Her entries were legendary and typically led to a nice bump in sales for a few months after the annual event."

I leaned back, closing my eyes to reflect on this new information. The pieces of this mystery were beginning to fall into place. A few pieces were obviously still missing, but I had a much better sense of what I was up against. Snapping my eyes open, the words tumbled out of my mouth.

"So what you're saying is that whoever left this anonymous note thinks that, if I don't enter, my sales will tank in the crucial holiday season and I'll be forced to shut down."

Tilda leaned forward, nodding excitedly. "Precisely! Which means..."

I finished her sentence for her, "I *have* to enter the Great Harvest Bake Off."

She clapped her hands and squealed in excitement.

"It sounds to me like your mind is made up."

"About entering? Yes, no question I have to. Except..."

"Except...what?"

"What beverage or beverages should I submit as entries?"

Tilda didn't waste a moment pondering my question.

"Definitely your cardamom latte. It's a new and unique drink that's already a village favorite."

"Done! How many beverages can each participant enter in the judging?"

"The rules state two entries per villager."

"Cocoa with a kick?"

Tilda shook her head. "I would advise against that choice. The judges wouldn't appreciate it. They have delicate palates that are not accustomed to spicy selections."

I raised my hand in the air, mimicking a pen scratching out an entry.

"Scratch that. Then what?"

I could almost see the wheels turning in Tilda's head. She bounced off the couch and high-tailed it to the kitchen. When she returned, she was leafing through *Betty's Steep Secrets*.

"Yes! Here it is!" She continued, when she noticed the look of confusion on my face. "Before your aunt died, she was working on a new entry: honey-thyme tea. The judges will look favorably on your nostalgic move if you honor her memory."

Tilda handed me the open recipe book before sitting

back down. I scanned the recipe and smiled. All of the necessary ingredients could be found in the shop. Our plan to thwart the mystery note sender was taking shape.

"The Bake Off is in two days. Should I make it now or morning of?"

"Now, definitely now. Betty always let her blends steep for a few days in the fridge before judging, choosing to heat them up just before leaving the shop. She said it allows the flavors to 'properly meld,' was how she phrased it."

I jumped up and headed toward the kitchen, with Tilda hot on my heels. Another thought stopped me in my tracks, causing Tilda to collide with me in a fit of giggles.

"Hang on. Don't I need to 'officially enter' before a deadline or something? That's how these competitions usually work."

Sensing my anxiety, Tilda placed a hand on each shoulder and took a deep breath. I followed her lead, inhaling and exhaling slowly. The action had its intended effect and I felt calmer.

"It's going to be okay, Rowan. Betty had already submitted her entry paperwork before she died. It just requires a quick conversation with the chair of the organizing committee to amend the name on Black Thumb Betty's entry."

"And who's that?"

"Hortense Slack."

No sooner had Tilda spoken her name, than the bell over the shop door chimed. Turning, Tilda whispered under her breath, "Speak of the devil."

19

Tilda pasted her warmest smile across her face, but to no avail. Hortense was spitting nails and looked ready for a fight.

"Hortense! What delightful timing you have. I was just explaining to Rowan that you could grant her permission to take Betty's place in the Bake Off beverage category."

A scowl still plastered across her face, Hortense's eyes were moving back and forth as she spoke.

"There will be no Bake Off if we don't get to the bottom of this."

She seemed to be scanning the shop, but for what we did not know.

"Bottom of what?" I inquired.

Hortense narrowed her eyes as she closed the distance between us. Holding an accusing finger in my face, she continued. "You! I warned you about hoarding spices."

I backed up slightly, to avoid a wagging finger being poked in my eye. Hortense's tone and accusation put me on the defensive and my response was just as heated.

"But I haven't bought any more cloves, or any other spices for that matter, since we last spoke."

Hortense turned on her heel and began stalking around the shop. She stopped in front of the herb cupboard and gasped. Her finger pointed at something we couldn't see from our vantage point.

Tilda and I stepped closer. Behind the large pestle and mortar was a paper bag stamped with the logo of Pennyworth's Provisions. A bag I had never seen before.

"I've never seen that bag before, Hortense."

She opened the glass door and retrieved the bag. Opening it up, we could all smell the contents: ground cloves. Hortense waved it in front of my face, sputtering her words at me.

"I warned you there'd be consequences if you continued to hoard clove. And now I have my proof!"

Tilda was like a mama bear, jumping to my defence. "Now, just one minute, Hortense. Rowan assured you she didn't purchase any spices, and I'm inclined to believe her."

Hortense then turned on Tilda. "Who said anything about purchasing? There was a break-in at Pennyworth's Provisions last night."

Tilda and I gasped in unison at Hortense's revelation.

"Oh dear! That's terrible and so unnerving for all shop owners in the village." I nodded along as Tilda spoke. "Rowan was at the pub with us last night, so it couldn't have been her doing."

Both women turned towards me as I smacked my hand against my forehead. "Cinnamon managed to get out of the shop last night because I didn't lock the door. He can open it if it's unlocked. I had to chase him down the garden path before I caught up. When we got back here, the shop door was ajar. At the time, I just assumed that was from his escape."

This bit of news caused a change in Hortense's demeanor. She lowered her hand and gingerly placed the bag on a nearby table. She stepped away from it as if it was dynamite. "If what you're saying is true,"

Nodding emphatically, I sputtered my response. "It is! I swear."

Unfazed by my interruption, Hortense continued. "If what you're saying is true, then that means someone may have planted this in your shop."

"To what end? Why would someone do that to me?"

Tilda filled in the missing blank. "To disqualify you from the Bake Off! Of course, that's what the mystery man meant about everything hinging on the Bake Off."

Hortense titled her head in confusion. "Mystery man? What are you blathering on about, Tilda?"

Tilda looked at me before responding. It was my mystery, so mine to share—or not—with Hortense. She was after all the village gossip, but in this case, I wondered if it could work in our favor. I shrugged as I responded to Tilda, "Can't hurt."

"Rowan received an anonymous note, telling her to leave the village. Last night, while rescuing Cinnamon, she heard a mystery man say everything would happen at the Bake Off."

Hortense grabbed her chest in shock. I quickly pulled out a chair and slid it behind her. Although our relationship had gotten off to a shaky start, the look on her face told me that she was now Team Rowan. As she sat down, she turned to me.

"What do you need from me?"

Her question was directed to me, but I allowed Tilda to

answer on my behalf. "Number one, approve her entry in the Bake Off. Number two, do what you do best as the 'village voice'." Tilda's euphemism was not lost on Hortense, but she nodded for her to continue. "Tell anyone and everyone that Rowan will be participating in this year's event in Betty's stead."

Hortense was nodding along, smiling as the idea that Tilda was spinning took shape. "You're hoping we can smoke out the culprit at the event!"

"That's exactly what I'm thinking! Now, day of, we'll need to keep our suspicions under wraps. We'll also need to keep extra eyes on Rowan."

Tilda's last comment got my attention and I bristled in response. "Are you suggesting that the note writer—or writers—mean me harm?"

Sensing my apprehension, the look on her face told me she immediately regretted her comment. Tilda wrapped me in a comforting hug, with Hortense reaching up to pat my exposed forearm. "Oh dear, I'm sorry I caused you any anxiety. All I meant was that they might confront you. Especially if their initial plan was to keep you from entering in the first place. They may be desperate and want to bully you into hightailing it out of the village."

Hortense took the opportunity to jump in, offering moral and practical support too. "Yes, we'll keep you safe, Rowan. I can even send Mortie over to be your stand assistant."

I felt much better knowing we had a plan and I had support. The moment made me feel like a fully-fledged member of the village.

Hortense closed the bag and stood up to leave. "Apologies for the misunderstanding. I should never have cast aspersions on your character, Rowan."

I placed my hands in a prayer position and bowed slightly. "Apology accepted. You were simply looking out for the village and its longstanding traditions. I would have done the same thing if I was in your shoes."

Following Hortense to the door, I turned the lock after closing it. Leaning against the door, I exhaled dramatically to express my relief. "Well, even if we don't know who left me the note, at least we have a plan to expose them at the Bake Off."

"Yes, one partial mystery solved. Now, should you get started on steeping the honey-thyme tea?"

I pushed myself off the door. Locking arms with Tilda, I guided us both towards the kitchen. "Great minds think alike! I was thinking the very same thing. And while the water boils, I'll fill you in on what I've anointed 'The Cinnamon Solution.'"

20

We were sitting at the kitchen table, tossing around ideas for Cinnamon. How could we administer a slow-release formulation that would allow Cinnamon to control when and for how long he could communicate with humans. Our conversation had practically bored the cat to tears. So much so, that he had slunk off to nap in the front alcove.

A cacophony of sounds interrupted our discussion: banging on the window, hisses from Cinnamon, and what could only be accompanying yips from Pudding and Pickles. The dog sounds were muffled. When we emerged from the kitchen, I discovered that they were on the sidewalk with my father.

My father caught my eye and waved furiously to get me to open the door faster. He was holding something in his hand, but I couldn't make it out from this distance. Before letting them in, I watched Tilda pick up a snarling Cinnamon. We were both still wary of his unfriendly reactions to the pugs.

"Dad, what's up? Why all the excitement?"

"Look what I found! Well, actually, what Pickles found."

He was still waving the object around, so I was having trouble identifying it.

"What is it?"

"A wallet, silly girl! It's a wallet."

"That must be Peter's!" I exclaimed.

Tilda and my father responded in unison. "Peter?"

I chuckled at their confused looks before filling them in. "Peter Bramble. He's a volunteer with the National Rambling Association, or NRA. He was walking along the village's garden path earlier this week. When I met him, it was getting dark and he told me that he'd lost his wallet and his car was over in Whiskerleigh."

"Gosh, that must have been a terrible shock for him. Where is he now?" My father inquired.

"Well, I got Gideon to open up his suite to Peter until he could get organized."

The gasp from Tilda shouldn't have surprised me given the events of the past month, but it did, nonetheless. "You, you...*spoke* to...*Gideon*? And...*he* spoke to *you*?"

I threw back my head in a hearty laugh, a gesture that felt oddly comforting after the stress of the past few days. "I did! He did! We behaved like grownups and I believe we even mended some fences."

Tilda returned Cinnamon to the couch so she could hug me once again. Her movements didn't go unnoticed by the pugs, who moved as one toward the couch. Without a noise, they laid down in front of Cinnamon. It was as if they were bowing to their leader. It almost seemed as if Cinnamon was smiling at this turn of events.

The scene shocked us into silence. It would need to be

unpacked at a later point, as my father cleared his throat and continued waving the wallet in the air. "So, is this Peter still in the village?"

"I believe so. But hang on, you never told us where you found it."

"We, I mean Pickles, loves snuffling around in fallen leaves. Autumn seems to be his favorite time of year."

My father was rambling, as was his wont. He certainly knew how to make a short story long. I raised my hand in a circular motion, encouraging him to move the story along.

"Right, yes. He was pushing his nose through the fallen leaves along the garden path when he pushed this onto the path. And I stepped on it."

Tilda clapped and turned towards the dog sporting the yellow leash. "Well done, you handsome lad."

I was bemused that Tilda could tell the difference between these near-identical canines. We had both only met them twenty-four hours earlier. Pickles was preening at the compliment, his tail wagging furiously, but he never wavered from his bowed position in front of Cinnamon. The cat seemed serene and almost regal with his newfound status.

"Hello? Earth to Rowan. What about Peter's whereabouts? Can I get his wallet to him? I checked the ID when I first picked it up, and judging by the address on his driver's license, home is quite far away."

Tilda floated towards my father, gently plucking it from his hand. "I have a better idea. Since Rowan has made peace with Gideon, I think it's time I act my age and do the same."

And with that, she was out the door and headed across Sycamore Row. My father took the opportunity to flop down beside Cinnamon on the couch.

"Coffee? Tea?" I asked.

"I'll have an herbal tea, if that's not too much trouble, my dear girl."

Glancing at the carafes lined up on the counter, I didn't see Betty's signature cinnamon-cardamom tea. I would need to brew a fresh batch, especially if I was leaving the door unlocked for customers.

"You got it, Dad! Give me ten or fifteen to brew a fresh batch. If any customers come in, please holler for me."

My father waved me away with his right hand. His left hand was gently stroking Cinnamon's back as I turned to the kitchen.

Just before the tea finished steeping, I heard the bell over the shop door chime. When no call from my father followed it, I figured Tilda had returned from her dual missions of wallet return and fence mending.

As I emerged with the tea, I was surprised to see Piper sitting on the floor with the pugs. She was chatting with my father, who appeared somewhat ill at ease.

"Piper, hi! I see you've met my father, Reginald Thorne. And Pudding and Pickles, of course."

"Your father? I thought you told me your parents were allergic to cats."

Piper's comment caused my father's face to turn a deep shade of red. He stopped petting Cinnamon and stood up. Pulling nervously at his collar, he seemed at a loss for words.

"That's right! How can you be in the same room as Cinnamon, let alone petting him? In all the excitement of your arrival, I totally forgot about that. Were you lying to me as a child?"

He closed the distance between us with two giant strides. Grabbing me by the shoulders, he looked me in the eye before responding. "It wasn't my idea, Rowan. To be honest, I was indifferent to getting you a pet. But your mother, well…"

"Well, what?" My impatience was growing.

"Well, she didn't want a pet. She knew all the work would fall to her."

"So instead of being honest with me, you both lied? To your only child?"

Needing space between us, I pulled away from my father. Turning to place the warm carafe of tea on the counter, my mind was racing a mile a minute. My father followed me to the counter, heading behind it so he could once again face me.

He held his fingers up as he emphasized his explanation with air quotes. "She framed it as a 'creative explanation.' She was 'allergic' to the idea of taking care of a cat."

I turned away from him yet again, this time heading to the front alcove and sank down into the couch next to Cinnamon. For once, he reacted to me in a comforting manner, gingerly placing his paw on my forearm. I covered his paw with my outstretched hand, squeezing it in acknowledgement. "What *other* secrets are you keeping from me? And why aren't you suffering from it?"

"Suffering? Whatever do you mean?"

"When I'm forced to keep secrets, I develop hives, lose sleep, and struggle to keep my lips sealed. You, on the other hand, seem completely unbothered by this decades-long secret."

My father approached cautiously and knelt down in front of me. His voice took on a more circumspect tone. "Your mother was so adamant that it was the right decision. I guess I convinced myself that it wasn't a lie and that the secret was worth keeping to maintain harmony in our family."

My shoulders relaxed, softened by my father's pleading expression. I looked from him to Piper, sitting side-by-side on the floor. She had kindly chosen to remain silent during our family drama. Their faces mere inches away from each other allowed me to examine them closely. To compare them. A feeling of familiarity was forming in my brain. I was beginning to believe that one of the mysteries occupying my grey matter would be solved in the not-too-distant future.

Just then, Tilda reentered the shop, an effusive smile lighting up her entire face. Looking from my father to Piper and back again, the same thought of familiarity seemed to be dawning on her.

"Oh? *Ohhhh*!"

I jumped off the couch and grabbed her hand, dragging her towards the kitchen. She came only partially willingly, dragging her feet as she turned to observe the two of them. Piper looked confused, while my father looked like he knew the jig was up.

Once behind the closed door, I grilled her almost immediately. "You know?!"

She turned my own words on me. "You know? How long have you known?"

"My suspicions began when I first met Piper."

"Not Petunia? I thought you met her first, at Arthur's London office."

I began pacing as I responded. "I did, but she was giving off weird vibes. In retrospect, I suspect it was because of that whole recipe book debacle. So, you know too?"

Tilda swept her hand in front of her. "It's as plain as day when you see them side-by-side."

I stopped pacing and looked at her. "It is, isn't it? I look more like my mom than my dad, so it took me a hot minute to put the pieces together." Then I started pacing again.

"What do I do? What do I say? 'Hi, Piper and Petunia. I'm your long-lost half-sister.'"

Tilda pursed her lips, holding her hands up to her face as she thought through that scenario. Steepling her index fingers against her lips, she scrunched her eyes closed and let out a weighty breath. "No, I don't think that's the best course of action."

I shook my head in disbelief. "Of course it's not. But how do I approach it? I can't put the toothpaste back in the tube."

"I think you need to speak to your father first. Find out the circumstances that led to this."

"By *this*, you mean fathering two secret children?"

"Well, when you put it like that, it sounds so..."

"True?"

"I was going to say lewd. But yes, I suppose it's also true."

Tilda approached me, clearly believing I needed a hug. She wasn't wrong and I didn't fight it when she wrapped her arms around me. "You need to give your father the benefit of the doubt. Let him share his side of the story and decide how and when he wants to tell the twins."

Tilda's last comment shook me out of my sorry-for-myself attitude. "You're right! Judging from Piper's interaction with him, she has no idea he's their father. You make a lot of sense."

Tilda giggled as she attempted to break the tension with a little levity. "You could say I'm wise beyond my years."

I didn't laugh at her self-deprecating joke, but it still had the intended effect.

"You're right. Of course you're right. But how do I do that?" I pulled away from Tilda and raised my arm, pointing towards the door. "I invited Piper over today. I can't just turn around and ask her to leave."

Tilda turned me around by the shoulders. She gently

pushed me through the swinging doors. Following close behind, she whispered in my ear.

"I can ask Piper to join me in the kitchen. We'll continue working on The Cinnamon Solution."

I nodded in agreement. Tilda's plan would work. I hoped.

21

After Piper and Tilda retreated to the kitchen, Cinnamon raised his head towards me. How could this cat possibly know what I was thinking? I pondered to myself. The look in his eyes told me all I needed to know.

With a subtle meow, he hopped off the couch and headed to the cat door into the kitchen. Pudding and Pickles seemed to understand Cinnamon's singular sound, standing up and following him through the cat door.

Now that we had the shop to ourselves, I decided we needed to maintain our interruption-free zone. Without a word, I opened the shop door, dragged the sandwich board inside, and locked the door behind me.

My father watched my movements soundlessly. I suspected he was waiting for me to speak first. Sitting on the couch, I patted the seat beside me. Once he had settled himself, I opened my mouth to speak. But the look on his face stopped me in my tracks. Closing my mouth, I leaned over and hugged him, a gesture he returned tenfold. His crushing hug was making it difficult to breathe.

"Dad. Can't. Breathe." I laughed to show him it was a good problem to have.

"Apologies, dear. I think I know what you want to ask me. I will answer all your questions truthfully."

Taking a deep breath, I closed my eyes to focus my thoughts. Clearly, my father was chastised by my discovery. I decided now was the time for information, not blame or shame.

"Okay, thanks. Are you Piper and Petunia's father?"

He chuckled nervously before staring off into the distance while he gathered his thoughts. That mannerism was one that had first raised my suspicions. He looked so much like the twins in that moment.

"In a manner of speaking."

What the heck did that mean? I held my tongue, waiting for my father to continue his explanation.

"Yes, I am their biological father. But I have never met either of them before today."

"Is that why you wanted to visit me? To see your other children?"

Visibly shaken by my questions, my father jumped up and began pacing.

"I came to see *you*, Rowan. That was my plan all along. But when you started telling me about your growing friendship with Piper and Petunia, I was worried you'd figure it out without knowing all the background information."

I took a breath before responding, not wanting to inflame my father during his vulnerable confession. "Well, I had my suspicions, but it wasn't until I saw you sitting beside Piper that I knew for sure."

"You are very perceptive, my dear Rowan. You're a testament to your aunt, she would have been so proud of your skills."

My father's comment confused me, and I tilted my head and shrugged my shoulders in response. What skills? Was he trying to change the subject? I kept quiet, hoping he would continue with his explanation. He did not disappoint.

"You see, Elspeth and I were good chums at uni. I knew her husband too, but that was long before they married. After I moved to America, we kept in touch. But only sporadically. This was before the entire world was connected twenty-four/seven. Back then, it was Christmas and birthday cards, with a few sentences at a time."

As my father spoke, he relaxed and stopped pacing. Sitting down beside me again, he took my hands in his. It was as if a weight had been lifted off his shoulders with his dual confessions. I nodded to indicate he should continue.

"Elspeth wrote one year that her husband was impotent and she was heartbroken that she couldn't have a child of her own. With that letter, my fate was sealed. I hopped on the next plane."

"So, you were...their sperm donor?"

"Yes! Nothing more and nothing less. I was helping out a friend. We felt it would be better for family unity—theirs and ours—if we kept it under wraps."

This last statement caused me to sit upright and interject. "So, Mom never knew."

He shook his head before responding. "We had only just met and I feared it may scare her away. I already knew she was the woman I would marry, and I didn't want to give her any reason to doubt my love and devotion to her."

My father exhaled forcefully, leaning back and closing his eyes. "I didn't realize how much this secret was weighing on me."

"I can imagine! I'm juggling a few of my own at the moment."

His eyes popped open and he looked at me with the look of a concerned parent.

"Care to share? As you can see, I'm quite good at maintaining confidences."

His nervous laugh did nothing to convince me. My secrets were mine to keep. "Thanks, but no. I promised certain people that I would keep my lips sealed. So, what's next? Are you going to tell Piper when she emerges from the kitchen?"

He shook his head vigorously. "It's not my story to share. First, I would need to visit Elspeth. From what Piper was just telling me, her dementia is already advanced. She may not even remember me."

I too shook my head. "I'm not so sure about that. She seems to have quite a firm grasp on the distant past. But I take your point. Maybe I should send Piper home with a double dose of Recollection Restorative and then we could visit later this evening. That is, if you want me to?"

My father's next words were interrupted by a commotion near the kitchen doors. Tilda had emerged and was holding open the swinging doors for a parade of prancing, talkative animals. In the lead, Cinnamon, head held high, was walking in a most royal fashion. He was followed closely by equally exuberant pugs.

"The feline king has left the kitchen. Subjects, secure the perimeter."

Pudding and Pickles were falling over themselves as they spread out in the shop. Pudding answered first. "Yes, my liege."

Pickles ran towards the front door, yelling in response. "Your wish is our command."

Piper took up the rear, giggling uncontrollably at the scene playing out in front of her. I clapped my hands and jumped off the couch, heading towards the unusual procession. "Is Cinnamon wearing...a collar?"

Tilda jumped in to explain. "Not a collar, per se. I fashioned a temporary device with a cut up tea towel and a cloth soaked in your latest cinnamon concoction. It will work for now."

Cinnamon interrupted our conversation with an impatient throat-clearing. "If you please, I request you vacate my alcove so I can commence my grooming ritual."

My father snorted as he laughed and jumped off the couch. Bowing to Cinnamon, he backed away like a true subject of royalty.

We watched the animal procession head to the couch as Tilda continued explaining their breakthrough. "As I was saying, Piper came up with the brilliant idea of a collar for Cinnamon."

Piper jumped in excitedly. "Yes, if you leave it on a looser setting, you can attach a potpourri sachet inside. Then you have a homemade time-release collar for his majesty."

We all giggled at Piper's last comment. Cinnamon was lapping up all the attention, especially the pugs bowing in front of him. They were still muttering—in English—to each other and Cinnamon.

I held up my hand to get the attention of the humans in the room. "What gives with the pugs? How come they're talking too?"

Tilda jumped in to answer my question. "As I was attaching the tea towel around Cinnamon's neck, they both kept rubbing up against him. This 'Cinnamon Solution' of yours must work on different animal species."

Cinnamon started scratching his ear, which caused the loosely tied tea towel to dislodge. "Hey! My collar is falling off. Humans, some assistance?"

Tilda and I both approached the bossy feline and examined the falling towel.

I gently tightened the knot. "We'll need a more permanent solution than this."

Piper rushed over to provide some much-needed advice. "You can purchase a cat collar at Pennyworth's Provisions. While you're there, also get a few potpourri sachets. You can put the 'Cinnamon Solution' in that and attach it to the inside of the collar."

"That's a great idea, Piper! I'll head there right away."

Piper glanced at her watch and headed to the door. "Shoot! I told Petunia I wouldn't be too long. She'll need a break from watching both the shop and Mum."

Grabbing Piper's arm gently, I slowed her progress to the front door. "Hang on, Piper. Before you go, I have something for your mother. Give me a sec to grab it from the kitchen."

I was back in a flash, carrying a large carafe of cold Recollection Restorative.

"This is a much stronger batch. It's been cooled in the fridge for a few days, so your mother can drink it any time, day or night."

Piper ran over to hug me before taking the carafe. "Rowan, thank you so much. I don't know what we'd do without you!"

I glanced over at my father. He was swiping a tear from his cheek. This display of affection between two of his three daughters had made my stiff-upper-lip British father emotional. And, judging from the smile blooming across his face, thrilled. He cleared his throat, causing us all to turn towards him.

"Piper, if you wouldn't mind terribly, I would like to visit your mother later today. Perhaps after the shops close?"

"Oh? Why's that?"

"Well, you see..."

My father was having difficulty forming words, so I jumped in to help him out. "How crazy is this? It turns out your mother and my father attended university together."

Piper's eyes grew large as she smiled. "Wow! What a small world! I knew there was a reason I liked you."

You have no idea, Piper, I thought to myself. Crossing my fingers behind my back, I hoped this secret would be a short-lived one. Judging from the look of relief on my father's face, I believed my assessment to be correct. "I'll come too. That way, I can see for myself how this stronger batch of Recollection Restorative is impacting your mother."

"Okay! It's a date then. Just head on over when you close up for the day."

I waved as Piper unlocked the door and wandered out on to Sycamore Row. She waved as she turned left, heading towards Lover's Lane. The sky had turned black since she first arrived, so she was jogging against the pellets of rain.

Turning to Tilda and my father, I motioned for them to follow me into the kitchen. The animals seemed consumed in their own drama, and I wanted an uninterrupted conversation.

Tilda astutely waited for me to "officially" fill her in on what we had both already known. She even had the presence of mind to appear shocked, but I wasn't sure we were fooling my father. "Well! It certainly has been an eventful day. Would you like me to pop over to Pennyworth's Provisions to pick up the collar and sachets?"

"Thanks for the offer, Tilda. But I think I should go myself. I want to ensure there are no lingering suspicions about the theft of clove."

Tilda nodded and offered a seat to my father. She turned towards the stove, picking up the kettle.

“Understood. I’ll brew us a spot of tea and confer with your father. He can be an added layer of support at the Bake Off.”

“What’s this now?” Tilda’s comment had piqued my father’s curiosity.

“I’ll fill you in while we enjoy our tea. *A lot* transpired while you were out finding wallets.”

I left them to it, their laughs following me out the shop door.

22

The rain had picked up since Piper's departure. Instead of turning back for an umbrella, I opted to run the short distance to the general store. A choice, in retrospect, that resulted in good and bad outcomes.

The wet leaves made the sidewalk slippery, a fact I only realized as I took a header in front of Smeaton and Sons Butchery. Smarting from the pain in my left knee, I sat back, leaning against the wall to recover. Rubbing my knee and looking down, I heard muffled voices. Voices that appeared to be arguing.

From my vantage point, I could turn my head slightly and see in their shop without being seen. What I saw was partly shocking, but at the same time, no surprise at all. Lewis Culpepper was pointing an accusatory finger at Chase and Hunter. He was so worked up, it looked like froth was dribbling out the sides of his mouth.

Chase seemed unfazed by his outburst, while his brother looked more concerned. Could these three be the culprits behind the anonymous note? It was looking more and more that way. My knee was feeling a bit better and I knew I had to move before Lewis left the shop.

The moment felt spy novel worthy, so I rolled on my left side. I army-crawled on my forearms until I was well away from their shop window. Springing to my feet, I forgot about my sore knee as I sprinted the rest of the way to Pennyworth's Provisions.

Tumbling in the door, I was soaked to the bone and panting heavily. Mrs. Pennyworth rushed over when she heard the commotion. She was an old-school shopkeeper who preferred formality. As such, I don't think most villagers knew her first name, myself included. She appeared to prefer it that way.

When she saw the state of me, she turned on her heel and retrieved something from under the counter. A pile of towels was in her arms as she approached me. Smiling, I reached out to accept one of the towels. Instead of handing one to me, she walked past me and began laying them on the wet floor. Once most of them had been used, she grudgingly handed the smallest one to me.

"I wish you young people would consult the weather before venturing out. You're not the first person to make such a mess in my shop. And it pains me to say, you won't be the last."

I wiped at my face and hair before handing the towel back to her. She retrieved it with the tips of her index finger and thumb, holding it away from her body as she returned to her perpetual spot behind the counter.

"Apologies, Mrs P., I didn't realize how heavy the rain was until I was out the door. Since our shops are so close, I thought I'd be okay. But then I slipped and ended up in the rain for longer than I had anticipated."

Mrs. Pennyworth tsk-ed as she shook her head. "That's

no problem of mine, Ms. Thorne. And I urge you to state your business and remove your dripping self from my shop as soon as possible."

She was a no-nonsense, no chit chat kind of woman. I took a deep breath and got right to the point.

"Well, I'm here for two reasons. First, I need to purchase a collar for Cinnamon and several potpourri sachets."

Mrs. Pennyworth set about gathering the supplies I requested, not waiting to hear my second reason for being in the shop. She plunked them on the counter and rang up the total on her cash, choosing to point at the total displayed instead of speaking. I fished in my pocket for the necessary bills and quietly placed them on the counter. Once I had my change and items in hand, she spoke again.

"And? What's the second reason?"

"Have you spoken to Hortense recently?"

"Mrs. Slack? Why would I speak to that vile woman?"

Such an odd comment, considering Hortense went out of her way to protect the supply of spices stocked on Mrs. Pennyworth's shop shelves. The relationships in this village still eluded me, but I didn't have time to unpack it right now. I soldiered on, unsure how Mrs. P. would react.

"I wanted to ensure you knew that I had nothing to do with the break-in last night. I did not steal your supply of clove."

Mrs. Pennyworth snorted as she replied. "A day late and a penny short, Ms. Thorne. I know all about the thief in question. They will get their comeuppance."

I was off the hook, but I didn't feel the relief I was hoping for. Mrs. Pennyworth crossed her arms and looked down her nose at me. Judging from her stance, our conversation was over and she was waiting, impatiently, for me to leave the shop. I took the hint and turned on my heel, opting to forego a farewell.

Back on the street, I once again sprinted towards Black Thumb Betty's. This time, though, I made sure to avoid piles of wet leaves, lest I take another tumble. As I passed Smeaton's, a quick glance in told me that Lewis had left the building. I heaved a sigh of relief, thankful that I had gotten off the sidewalk before then.

Tumbling through the shop door, I laughed at the expressions on my father's and Tilda's faces at the state of me. I must have looked like a drowned cat, and I felt that way too. Tilda rushed over to retrieve the collar and sachets from me. Instead of leading me to the couch, she marched me to the secret staircase that led right into my suite.

"You, young lady, are in need of a hot shower and dry set of clothes. I will hold down the fort while you get yourself sorted."

I nodded in agreement, happy to have her looking out for me. My father was great, but a woman's touch was what I needed right now.

Before heading upstairs, I paused by the kitchen door. The three animals were yelling over each other in the kitchen. They seemed quite excited with their newfound voices.

23

Rolling over on my side, it took me a minute to get my bearings. I must have fallen asleep after my shower. The room was pitch dark, as the sun had set several hours earlier. Switching on the bedside light, I sat up and stretched.

Murmured voices downstairs told me that my father had kept Tilda company in the shop.

I padded toward the internal staircase, careful to avoid that fifth, creaky step on my way down. If the animals were sleeping, I didn't want to wake them unnecessarily. I suspected their earlier excitement may have worn off.

Shaking my head, I marveled at the scene that had unfolded, and it was nothing I had expected. None of them were, in fact, sleeping. Instead, I was rewarded with a most wonderful scene: a cat and two dogs, speaking words and interacting with the humans in the room. Cinnamon was clearly in charge, a fact that seemed right as rain with Pudding and Pickles. And Cinnamon, for that matter.

Tilda had encouraged them to retreat to the kitchen, lest an unsuspecting customer enter the shop and discover what we had been trying to keep a secret. Cross-species communication was definitely a challenging concept to process. I wasn't sure some of the villagers were prepared to accept it. Until we knew otherwise, this secret would have to remain amongst the select few who were in the know: members of the Catmint Council, Piper and her family, and my father.

Tilda looked up as I entered the room. "Hello, sleepyhead! We decided to give you some quiet time to recuperate. Reginald was kind enough to assist me with the closing activities. So, the two of you are good to go with your visit to Blooming Brews."

I smiled appreciatively at my friend before squeezing my father's extended hand. Neither of us was sure how the evening would unfold, but we were in this together. Tilda had offered to take the pugs for a walk and nature break after locking up the shop. My father had given her his room key so she could drop them back at the inn when she was ready to head to Arthur's.

Out on Sycamore Row, we bid Tilda, Pudding, and Pickles adieu as we turned left and they turned right. The pugs already knew the route to the garden path, so they were gently but firmly pulling Tilda along. One of her signature giggles escaped her lips as she allowed herself to be led by them.

"Bye! Have fun you three," I hollered after them before hooking my arm with my father's.

He was exuding a nervous energy that I had never seen in him before. I couldn't say that I blamed him, though. Neither of us knew how this evening would unfold. We were opening up a can of worms for the entire Bloom family.

Our footsteps fell into a steady rhythm as we rounded the corner onto Lover's Lane. It felt like I was five years old again, and we were heading on an adventure. The thought made me laugh, an infectious sound that seemed to soothe my father's nerves.

We arrived in front of Blooming Brews just as Petunia was turning the sign to closed. She smiled at me but seemed oddly confused when she looked at my father. Maybe she saw the resemblance too. We'd soon find out, I decided.

"Come in, come in. Piper told me you'd be stopping by. Hi there, Mr. Thorne, I'm Petunia."

My father grasped her extended hand, chuckling nervously. "Please, Reginald, or even Reg. My father was Mr. Thorne."

"Sure thing, Reg it is. You know, Mum used to mention an old classmate named Reg."

Still holding Petunia's hand, my father began shaking it up and down in time with his nodding head. "Yes! That's me! I'm Reg from uni."

Petunia pulled her hand away, gingerly rubbing her shoulder in the process. It seemed my father's exuberance was a little too much for her. "What a small world! The Bloom and Thorne families have past history predating COW."

"Indeed we do. Indeed we do. Is Elspeth about? I was hoping to say hello."

Petunia turned around and hollered towards the back of the store. "Mum! Piper! We have company."

Piper emerged, followed by her mother. Elspeth's demeanor seemed more alert this evening. I was hoping they had given her an extra dose of Recollection Restorative before our arrival. Judging from the look on Elspeth's face when she laid eyes on my father, the answer must have been yes.

"Oh my lord. Is it really you?"

My father closed the distance between them and picked

up Elspeth's hands. He squeezed them before planting a kiss on them. "It is. Hello, Elspeth. Long time, no see."

"Well, Reg, you always were one for subtlety. I would call that the understatement of the century."

Hands still clasped, the two of them walked to the nearest table. They opted to sit side-by-side on the bench so they could remain in close contact. Piper and Petunia looked confused, so I motioned for us to head to the back of the shop. I wanted the former classmates to have a few moments to themselves before the big reveal.

Piper was the first to break the silence. "Mum recognized Reg right away." Petunia and I nodded in agreement, allowing her to continue her thoughts. "And he seems to have a calming effect on her."

"It's the most alert I've seen her in a while," Petunia chimed in. "I'm sure your latest formulation is helping too, Rowan."

I smiled warmly at my sisters. "Happy to help any way I can."

Suddenly, I was feeling nervous about the impending reveal. I hoped it wouldn't negatively impact the growing friendship the three of us had been developing.

I was about to broach the topic with them when my father called us to the front of the shop. Still holding Elspeth's hand, I could sense that they had agreed to share the news together.

"Girls, ahem, apologies. Let me start again. Young ladies, would you kindly join us?"

The three of us shrugged as one and headed towards the pair. Sitting across from them, I had purposely wedged myself between my father and the twins. If there were any strong emotions bubbling to the surface in the coming minutes, I wanted to shield my father from possible slaps of fury. Hopefully, I was overreacting, but one could never be too sure.

Reg looked at Elspeth and nodded. She was going to deliver the news to her/their daughters. Unclasping her hands from Reg's, Elspeth reached across the table with her hands extended. Piper and Petunia each took one, turning to each other in confusion. They turned back towards their mother, waiting for her to speak. My father and I both leaned back, not wanting to intrude on the last moment they would have as a family of three.

"Dears, there's something important I need to tell you, but I'd like you to let me finish before you ask questions. Can you do that?"

Nodding mutely, the girls squeezed their mother's hands.

"Thank you, my loves. This may come as a shock to you, but the man you thought was your father was that in name only." Elspeth took a deep breath to steady her nerves. "You see, we discovered shortly after we married that your father couldn't have children. I was devastated, because I had always wanted to be pregnant and have a child—or, in your case, children—of my own."

Piper and Petunia looked shocked, but they allowed their mother to continue with her explanation.

"I had written a birthday card to Reg, who had moved to America by this time. One line at the bottom was all it took for him to fly over here and offer his help. And yes, by help I mean a sperm donation so I could conceive my own child."

Petunia could no longer hold her tongue. "But...what about Dad? Was he on board with this?"

"He was. You see, Reg and I were just friends at school. There was never a romantic relationship. When he offered this generous gift, the three of us sat down and worked out the technical aspects. That included drawing up a contract of agreement. Other than the three of us, the only people who knew were the doctor and nurse who performed the procedure. They agreed to maintain our confidentiality."

Piper and Petunia continued to hold their mother's hands but grabbed each other's too. This was a lot to take in, and they were handling it quite calmly. I glanced over at my father, who was mesmerized by the scene unfolding in front of him.

Piper took the opportunity to ask a question I'm sure Petunia was also wondering. "Does that mean Dad adopted us?"

"Not at all. He's listed on your birth certificates as your father, a title he was fiercely proud of up until the day he died."

Piper then turned to me. "Did *you* know?"

I shook my head vigorously. "Not at first. I had my suspicions. You two have some of the same mannerisms as my father. At first, I couldn't put my finger on it. Until..."

Piper jumped in, finishing my sentence. "Until I came to the shop today! I thought you had a funny look on your face, but I assumed it had to do with Cinnamon."

Nodding this time, I filled in the blanks. "That's right. As soon as I looked at you and Dad sitting beside each other, the resemblance was uncanny. But I needed to confirm it with him first. I didn't feel it was my place to blurt it out to you."

Piper seemed shocked but happy, while Petunia was having a more difficult time processing this new information. The entire situation seemed to be having an impact on their mother, whose face was transforming into one with a very confused look. Her glance at me confirmed my suspicions; this latest batch of Recollection Restorative was wearing off.

I turned towards Piper and raised my eyebrows. Nodding in agreement, she took charge. As she reached forward with her other hand, Piper spoke very slowly and gently to her mother.

"This has been a full and eventful day. I think we could all use a good night's sleep. That should give our brains adequate time to process our new reality."

Petunia didn't wait for her sister to finish speaking. She pulled her hand away from her mother's and stalked off.

Piper sighed and continued. "I'm sorry, Reg. It may take my sister a bit longer to accept you in our life."

My father waved his hands in the air, shaking his head from side to side. "No need to apologize in the least. We've dropped a lot on you in a short period of time. Rowan and I will say goodbye. I will leave it to you to reach out in the coming days."

Piper nodded and smiled, a look of relief washing over her face. My father and I rose as one, quietly heading towards the door. I turned and blew Piper a kiss. She reached up to grab it out of the air and put against her cheek. It was a good sign that our intertwined futures were beginning on a positive note.

24

A shiver rolled down my body as we exited Blooming Brews. The brisk autumn air was bracing, and I had forgotten to bring my coat. My father quickly removed his blazer and wrapped it around my shoulders. He turned me around by the shoulders, leaning down to look me in the eye.

"I'm so sorry, Rowan. I should have told you sooner."

I leaned against my father, wrapping my arms around his waist. It was partly for warmth, partly for moral support. Tilting my head, I smiled before standing on my tip toes to plant a kiss on his cheek.

"Look, I'd be lying if I didn't say it's a bit of a kick in the pants that you didn't trust me to tell me sooner. But, I'm an adult and I can hold two competing thoughts in my head."

He snorted out a laugh as he hugged me back.

"You are wise beyond your years, just like when you were a child."

I pulled away and linked my arm in his, leading him up Lover's Lane towards Sycamore Row.

"Don't get me wrong. I'm still upset with you. You'll need

to give me time, too, to process this change in our family makeup."

He nodded sagely, choosing his words carefully.

"Understood. That's the least I can do for you, not to mention Piper and Petunia."

We strolled along quietly, each lost in our own thoughts. It was a lot to take in: two new half-sisters! What did that make Elspeth to me? A stepmother? Nothing? My mind was swirling.

Feeling playful, I kicked a few leaves as I walked. The cool wind had dried the previously wet leaves. Suddenly, the urge to reach down and grab a handful overtook me. Picking them up, I threw them over our heads. My father picked up on my playfulness, grabbing me by the shoulders and spinning me around in the falling rainbow of color. All wasn't forgiven, but we were making progress.

Arriving at the shop, a note from Tilda was taped to the door.

Came back to the shop after our walk. Cinnamon was bossing the pugs around. Needed to maintain my sanity. Pugs are at the inn; I've returned to Arthur's.

Toodles,

Tilda

"Uh oh, maybe leaving the collar on Cinnamon was a mistake. I hope he wasn't too rude to Pudding and Pickles."

My father chuckled at my concern. "Nothing they can't handle, I'm sure. I'll say goodnight here and head to the inn."

My father once again embraced me in a hug; one I

returned lovingly. He turned and waved as he crossed Sycamore Row, picking up his pace when a car turned from Lover's Lane.

The car was traveling quite fast for the narrow road. I backed away from the road, fearful it might jump the curb. Instead, it skidded to a stop right beside me. It wasn't until Rory jumped out of the driver's seat that I realized it was Arthur's car.

"Rory! What a surprise. I'm just getting back from the Blooms' shop. Would you like to come in for a visit?"

He pulled off his driver's cap, his dark curls tumbling around his face. My heart skipped a beat when he smiled at me. Maybe I was developing feelings for someone I had previously just considered a friend. Shaking my head to clear that thought, I knew I had more important tasks at hand before I could consider a date.

"Only for a quick moment, Rowan. Arthur called me to drive him to London tonight. It seems there's an important meeting he must attend in person first thing in the morning."

I turned to unlock the door, realizing too late that Cinnamon was just inside the door. He began berating me for my late arrival.

"Well! It's about time you returned to the scene of the crime."

I quickly tried to back out the door, hoping Rory hadn't heard him talking. But it was too late. Rory was a full head taller than me. He was looking over me, a mischievous grin on his face.

"I knew it! Cinnamon *can* talk."

Shocked at his statement, I turned around and pulled him inside. Locking the door behind us, I picked up

Cinnamon and motioned for Rory to join me in the alcove. Cinnamon was none too pleased at my actions.

"Unhand me, woman! I refuse to be manhandled by the likes of you."

I dropped him rather unceremoniously beside me as Rory flopped into the chair opposite the couch.

"You know? How?"

"Mum. She cleans for the Reverend and heard a few heated exchanges at Catmint Council meetings."

The circle of people in the know was growing, and I had mixed feelings about it. My face must have betrayed the conflict I was juggling. Rory reached out and grabbed my hand, and I had to admit, it felt nice, as well as reassuring.

"It's okay, Rowan. Your secret is safe with me," he squeezed my hand at this point. I found myself squeezing back.

"*This* secret," I mumbled under my breath.

Rory looked at me quizzically, reaching his other hand across the table to snuggle Cinnamon. The cat was licking his fur, in an attempt to smooth down the section I had ruffled when I scooped him up.

"Something else on your mind? I'm a good listener, if you need to unload."

Exhaling through pursed lips, I removed my hand from his and leaned back. Raking my fingers through my hair, I felt a moment of weakness growing in my brain. Should I share Arthur's secret with him? What harm could it do?

Opening my mouth to speak, I was interrupted by Cinnamon.

"My bowls are empty. I am not amused."

The tension broken, Rory and I laughed at his outburst. The moment passed, and Arthur's secret remained behind the curtain for another day.

I motioned for Rory to follow me into the kitchen. A talking, demanding cat would not help us finish our conversation before Rory had to leave. Picking up his bowls, I turned to the sink. I was grateful to have a break from his piercing eyes on my face, but I still felt them on the back of my head.

I averted my gaze when I turned to the fridge. Retrieving Cinnamon's food, I once again turned my back on Rory. The food bowls replenished, I placed them under the table and whistled for Cinnamon.

"I know you're in a time crunch with Arthur. Can we continue this conversation when you return to the village?"

"You got it! And I'm serious, no one is going to hear about Cinnamon from me."

"Appreciate that. I need to fine tune the formulation in his collar before I let him loose on the world. I want him to be able to talk when he wants to, but not if it's going to jeopardize our stay in the village."

Rory waved at the mess on the kitchen table.

"Is that what you'll be working on tonight?"

I laughed awkwardly, realizing the kitchen looked like a complete disaster.

"I wish! No, I'm prepping some entries for the Great Harvest Bake Off. That's more time-sensitive than Cinnamon. I can just remove his collar if he keeps speaking out of turn."

Rory laughed too, turning towards the swinging doors before pausing. He looked like he wanted to say something but was struggling to form the words. Turning back to me, he had a wistful look in his eye.

"I'll make sure we're both back in time for the judging. You know, to support you and Black Thumb Betty's."

"That would be great! And most appreciated, of course."

I followed him into the shop, curious as to what he was holding back. He would tell me when he was ready, I supposed. Still sulking, Cinnamon hadn't come into the kitchen when I whistled. Rory stopped by the couch, swinging the feline into the air before pulling him towards his chest.

"Don't worry, pal. Your secret is safe with me. Mum's the word."

Cinnamon didn't seem to mind being manhandled by Rory. He placed a paw on his arm before responding. "And you have my word that *your* secret is safe with me. Period. End of story."

Rory threw his head back, laughing uproariously at Cinnamon's comment.

"Of course, you would have heard me confiding in Rowan about returning to run my parents' farm. Well, thanks then."

He waved to me and jogged out to the door. The car's wheels smoked as he screeched away, heading towards Arthur's country home.

Locking the door, I turned towards Cinnamon. "Tomorrow will be busy prepping for the Bake Off. Do I have your word that you'll keep the chatter under wraps when customers are about?"

He made his best attempt at a bow before one sarcastic word escaped his lips. "*Fine.*"

Relieved, I waved him towards the inner staircase before turning off the lights in the shop. It had been a long day indeed.

25

Friday
One Day Before the Great Harvest Bake Off

The next morning, the shop was a hive of activity. My father arrived with the pugs just as Piper entered, pulling her reluctant sister behind her. Petunia fell to the floor and began cuddling Pudding—or was it Pickles?—cooing as she scratched behind her ears.

The scene was interrupted by Tilda flowing in with an enormous grin lighting up her entire face. Clearly, something had transpired before Arthur's return to London but now was not the time to inquire. Tilda clapped her hands together to get everyone's attention.

"Listen up! We don't have much time. The Bake Off is tomorrow, and we need to ensure someone has eyes on Rowan at all times."

I had filled in Piper and Petunia upon their arrival, who had agreed to help with my stall. Though Blooming Brews had entered the Bake Off beverage category in the past, this year was different. Both women had been so focused on their mother's deteriorating condition, they opted to forego the contest.

My father spoke up first. "It goes without saying that I will be front and centre day of. Is there a dog sitter I can hire during the event?"

Petunia jumped to her feet before anyone had a chance to respond. "I'll do it!" She looked sheepishly at my father, then down at her feet. "That is, if you'll allow me to."

"I think it's a grand idea, Petunia. These two have taken to you and shouldn't cause you too much trouble."

He snorted a laugh out at his own comment, a sound that reverberated through the shop as both twins joined in. When they all realized they were making the same sound, it caused another round of snorting laughter to escape their lips. Nothing like a little pet diplomacy to smooth over an awkward situation, I thought.

It was Piper's turn to chime in. "The only thing Petunia loves more than dogs is little children. They'll be in great hands."

Petunia blushed as she smiled and looked down at the pugs. They were circling her feet, leashes in their mouths. Taking their cue, she attached the leashes and led them to the door. With a wave, she was off, being pulled along by the excited little pups.

Tilda corralled the rest of us into the kitchen. I had risen early to clean the kitchen and get started on Bake Off prep work. The table had several "prep stations" set up with various tasks.

We got to work immediately. My father filled a box with paper cups and napkins. Piper sat down and began drawing beautiful signs to promote Betty's honey-thyme tea and my cardamon latte. Tilda packed another box with a two-burner hot plate and special carafes that would keep the tea hot on site. I leaned against the counter, unsure how to help my efficient team of helpers.

Pulling my recipe book out of the drawer, I was pleasantly surprised that I now thought of it as mine. The latest blend of Recollection Restorative had been weighing on my mind, and I wanted to consult Betty's earlier notes. I was convinced it had helped Elspeth sleep, and that the good night's sleep had in part helped with her memory recall. It made me wonder if Recollection Restorative, and not Sleep Salve, would help Reverend Primrose.

I sat at the other end of the table, the only area with enough space to open the book and lay it flat. Tilda had been coaching me on Betty's shorthand—what she called her "cryptic note taking"—and it had unlocked many of the earlier recipes.

Flipping towards the front of the book, I leafed through a few pages before I found what I was looking for. I dragged my thumb down the page, muttering under my breath as I absorbed the words.

"A-ha! I knew it."

My outburst caused everyone to stop working and look towards me. They waited for me to fill in the blanks. I read a few more sentences before I felt ready to share my findings. It was speculation on my part, but I thought I was on to something.

"When I gave the new blend of Recollection Restorative to Elspeth and heard how well she slept, it reminded me of something Betty had written early on."

My father chimed in. "Oh? Do tell, dear."

"Well," I looked down again, my finger pointing to a section at the bottom of the page. "It says here that Betty had been testing this blend on herself. She writes here that this stronger formulation made her quite drowsy."

I flipped a few more pages, running my finger down this latest page. "And here, she says she lost consciousness after one too many cups of it."

My father rose from the table, walking to the end and sitting down beside me. "I'm not sure I'm following you, dear. What, exactly, do you know?"

"Well, maybe 'know' isn't the right word. I *believe* I know what caused Betty's death."

This statement caused Tilda and Piper to join us at the far end of the table. They clearly didn't want to miss a word of what I was about to say.

"Go on, Rowan," Tilda replied gently.

"Okay, here goes. I think Betty was drinking Recollection Restorative during her deep clean. Tilda, you told me Betty's memory was starting to slip too, and she had a vested interest in finding a solution for Elspeth."

"True, I did notice she was getting a tad forgetful."

"Well, what if she drank too much, started to feel faint, and grabbed the bookshelf to steady herself. They're not affixed to the walls, so she could have collapsed and accidentally pulled the bookshelf on top of herself."

Everyone sat quietly, reflecting on my theory. It was my father who reached out first, grabbing my hand. "I think you may be on to something here. Betty's death was an unfortunate accident, not a case of foul play."

We all nodded and bowed our heads, thinking about Betty's final moments and untimely death. Our reflection was interrupted by Cinnamon barreling through the cat door. He looked at each of us in turn and, satisfied everyone already knew his secret, began barking out demands.

"You're late with refreshing my bowls. I want warm milk and honey to drink, not any herbal slop."

I arose as we all laughed at his outburst. "The master has spoken. I'll let you all get back to your stations, and I'll get his food and drink sorted."

Cinnamon sat back on his haunches, glaring down his nose haughtily at me. I giggled as I picked up my pace and reached down for his bowls. I got the milk and honey steeping on the stove before turning to his food bowl. If he could have tapped his foot impatiently, I'm sure he would have.

"She's pouring the milk. She's placing it on the floor."

He was narrating my movements, a feature of a talking cat I could do well without. When I finally placed the warm milk and honey in front of him, he took one slurp and stepped back.

"The milk is lukewarm. I disapprove."

I interjected with a rhetorical question, sarcasm dripping from my voice. "Isn't this fun?"

Piper saved me when she approached and whispered something in my ear. Nodding, I reached down and deftly removed the collar from his neck. We turned away from him as she continued whispering in my ear. Nodding to me, she turned and left the shop in a flurry of activity.

"What's the story, morning glory?"

"Well, Dad, we can't have Cinnamon blurting out comments at inappropriate times. We also can't have him narrating our every move. It will get real tiresome, real fast."

My father nodded. "Agreed. So what's the plan?"

"Piper just read about a collar limiter that is gentle for animals."

"Doesn't a limiter deliver electric shocks to dogs when

you're training them? That seems a bit excessive, you could just remove the collar."

I shook my head before continuing. "No, this new one doesn't deliver shocks. It just vibrates, so the animal pays attention to the vibration. Piper thinks the vibration will be enough to convince Cinnamon to curb his tongue, without harming him or causing him any distress."

"That does sound like an intriguing solution."

"And it's only temporary. Just until Cinnamon learns the social etiquette of speaking with humans on a regular basis."

My father smiled and clapped. "Then I approve on Cinnamon's behalf. Wouldn't want anyone hurting this magnificent feline."

"Agreed. And there's good news for you too!"

My father tilted his head. His hand stopped in midair, a pile of paper cups tumbling out of it. I laughed as I walked over to help him pick them up.

"Piper thinks the collar with the limiter and special herbal formulation will help Pudding and Pickles too."

Tilda squealed with delight. "That *is* good news! I shall enjoy hours of delightful dialogue with those two lovelies."

Her enthusiasm was infectious and my father and I joined in. Although I was extremely nervous about my appearance at the Bake Off the next day, these moments of levity were easing my mind. I knew I wouldn't sleep tonight, that was a given with my current level of anxiety. But I was hopeful that everything would be resolved in the next day and a half.

26

Saturday
Day of the Great Harvest Bake Off

The morning of the Bake Off, I was a ball of nervous energy. True to form, I had tossed and turned all night. It was before dawn, but I got up anyway, anxious to get this day started. If Tilda was right, the sender—or senders—of the anonymous note would reveal themselves at the village event.

I headed to the kitchen, to brew some very strong coffee and complete the last-minute preparations. Tilda, Piper, and my father were due in an hour. They would help me carry all the supplies to the Community Hall. It would be transformed into a market space for the Bake Off, with each entrant receiving a table for their wares. Local children had decorated the walls with autumnal scenes: lots of colorful leaves, pumpkins, and scarecrows. The judges would sit at the front of the hall, on the dais normally reserved for Village Council members during meetings.

While I waited for my coffee to brew, I cleaned Cinnamon's bowls and refreshed his food and drink. I didn't have the energy for a repeat of yesterday's spectacle with the cat. Piper had returned empty-handed from the vet clinic in Whiskerleigh. The gentle, no-harm collar limiters were on back order.

I had decided to leave Cinnamon in the shop with his collar affixed. He could talk his heart out to no one in particular. All shops in the village were closed so participants, judges, and villagers alike could attend the Great Harvest Bake Off.

Sipping my coffee, I wandered into the shop. I unlocked the door so my volunteer helpers could enter at their leisure. I had no worries about customers, since everyone would be saving their appetites for the Bake Off entries.

As I turned towards the kitchen, the bell above the shop door chimed. Turning, I was surprised to see that it wasn't one of my Bake Off helpers entering the shop. Instead, it was Gideon Place, looking halfway between nervous and awkward.

"Gideon! I'm surprised to see you so early this morning. Are you looking to buy a drink before the Bake Off?"

He hesitated before speaking. "No-o-o-o, not at all. I'm here on a different matter."

"Oh?"

Wringing his hands together, he began babbling a mile a minute. "You see, I owe you an apology."

"What for? I thought we had resolved everything when I introduced you to Peter Bramble and he agreed to pay to rent your suite."

He shook his head vigorously. "It's about my wife, Ellie. I

shouldn't have yelled at you when you were only just trying to help her."

I waved my free hand in the air as I spoke. "Water under the bridge. You were only looking out for your family."

"True. But not very well, it would seem."

"Whatever do you mean?"

"Ellie told me she came to you as she had been coming to your aunt in the past. You see, before we left Scotland, she had both our mothers to help with the children. They're a lot and she's been doing it all on her own."

"Wow, with four young children at home, that must be exhausting for her."

He nodded before lowering his head. "And I'm ashamed to say I have been so busy with the pharmacy that I didn't notice."

An idea began to form in my head. "Yes, as a fellow shop owner, I understand how busy it can be running a business. What I'm hearing is that Ellie needs help with the children and you don't have the capacity to chip in."

He nodded sadly. "Quite right, Rowan. I feel like I am failing as a husband and a father."

"Hang on there! You can't be in two places at once. I have an idea of how we can help your wife."

Gideon's face lit. "You do? What is it?"

"Well, I don't want to spill the beans until I know it'll work. Are they planning to attend the Bake Off today?"

My excitement was infectious, and Gideon began nodding his head excitedly. "Yes, they are. Why do you ask?"

"Before the judging begins, bring them all to my booth. I'm hoping the solution will present itself. Now if you'll excuse me, I need to prepare. It's a big day for me!"

Gideon smiled and nodded, backing towards the door. I waved at him before returning to the kitchen with my empty cup. I decided to start moving the boxes from the kitchen to the front of the shop while I waited for everyone to arrive.

Cinnamon descended the inner staircase just as I placed the last box by the door. He seemed well rested. I wouldn't know his level of feistiness until he began speaking.

"Hey bud. Today's the big day. If it's okay with you, I'd rather you keep an eye on the shop while I'm at the Bake Off. You know, in case the anonymous note senders decide to drop off another threatening note."

Crossing my fingers behind my back, I hoped he wouldn't discover my little white lie. It was partially true, I did want someone here just in case. But I also wanted to limit his time around villagers, lest he begin speaking.

Since he had been wearing the collar last night before going to sleep, I no longer needed to reach for a jar of cardamom pods or a stick of cinnamon to get a response from him.

"As you wish. If they do darken our door, I will deliver a proper tongue-lashing."

I laughed nervously, unsure how I felt about this new version of Cinnamon. Vocal *and* belligerent.

"Great, glad we're on the same page. Your bowls are cleaned and refreshed, so I hope you enjoy your breakfast."

"I shall." He responded as he strode majestically towards the cat door.

Just like the previous day, everyone seemed to arrive at once. Petunia immediately rushed over and grabbed the leashes from my father.

"See you before the judging!" She hollered before racing out the door with the yapping pups.

The rest of us converged on the boxes at the door. It would take us a few trips to carry everything that would be needed. I was pleased for the assistance and was feeling confident that my unknown nemesis wouldn't confront me enroute to the Bake Off.

"Safety in numbers," I muttered to myself.

Tilda's lilting voice startled me back to the present moment. "What's that, dear?"

"Oh, nothing important. Just wondering how things will go today."

She put down the box she had been juggling on her hip and patted my shoulder. "We're all here for you. Whoever left the note won't have the opportunity to chase you out of town."

"That's right," Piper chimed in. "They've met their match!" She flung her hands in the air, mimicking karate chops as she spouted nonsensical fighting sounds. The entire spectacle lightened my mood and I laughed immediately.

"Thanks, all of you. I don't know what I'd do without you!"

Tilda reached back down to retrieve the box. "You'd be late, that's what. Now, let's get this train moving. The Bake Off rules state you must have your stall set up before the doors open to the public. Chop, chop!"

And with that, our train of box carriers trudged out of Black Thumb Betty's, across Sycamore Row, and down past the Hare & Harrow.

The decor in the Community Hall was festive and seemed to be putting all those assembled in a friendly mood. The energy in the room was harmonious and uplifting. I was excited to be participating in my first-ever Great Harvest Bake Off.

Once my team had helped me set up, they huddled in the corner. The trio of Piper, Tilda, and my father agreed that my father would begin the morning as my helper. The other two would wander around, playing the role of villagers attending the Bake Off, as opposed to the "undercover spies" they truly were that day.

Hortense whistled from across the room. She and Mortimer were behind the Copper Kettle's entry table, displaying Hortense's famous pumpkin muffins and apple crumble. Hortense pointed at her husband and then her watch. I nodded and held up three fingers to indicate he should relieve my father in three hours. She nodded back and turned around, just as the doors were opened to the public.

Although she was on the judging panel, that didn't stop her from entering her own baked goods in the contest. Nobody wanted to point out the unevenness of her judging her own entries. Picking a fight with Hortense was like picking a fight with a porcupine: prickly and painful.

The next few hours passed quite quickly for my father and me. Both of my entries were equally popular with villagers, so we saw a brisk business. It helped to distract my mind from a potential run-in later in the day. I was busy ringing up a sale for Moira Culpepper when a hubbub at the front entrance caught the attention of almost everyone in the Community Hall.

Stan Pigeon was backing into the hall, followed by both Smeaton sons, and Lewis Culpepper. They were being corralled through the door by a motley crew: Cinnamon, Pudding and Pickles, followed lastly by Petunia. She was out of breath and attempting to reach for the pugs' leashes.

I ran over as Stan, shaking like a leaf, hurled insults at Cinnamon.

"Stay away, you mangy creature! I have a knife and I'm not afraid to use it."

I was about to interject when Cinnamon spoke up to defend himself.

"Try me, mailman."

He had spoken! In front of most of the village. As I looked around the room, I was taken aback by the lack of shock from the assembled crowd. Another mystery that would have to wait for now. I rushed over to Cinnamon and picked up him.

"Are you sure you want to be speaking right now?" I whispered in his fur.

"It's *fine*, Rowan. This is more important."

And with that, he jumped out of my arms, circling the four men. With a nod to the pugs, he stopped in front of Lewis. Pudding and Pickles each took a spot on the floor in front of Chase and Hunter, growling menacingly. The action had its intended effect, as both Smeatons were frozen in place. I turned to Petunia with a puzzled look on my face.

"What happened?"

"We were heading back towards Black Thumb Betty's, and I saw the four of them," she pointed at the men in question, "arguing at the front entrance. Stan had a letter in his hand but wouldn't push it through the slot. Lewis grabbed it from him and was about to when..."

Cinnamon took over from Petunia. "When I opened the door and took chase. I called to Pudding and Pickles, 'Now! Close the flanks—don't let anyone bolt.' We maintained formation and drove them right into your clutches."

Cinnamon sat back, nodding again to the pugs. They followed his lead and sat back on their haunches too. I walked up to Lewis, who was still clutching the undelivered letter. Holding out my hand, he grudgingly handed it to me.

"What does this say, Lewis? Are the four of you behind the threats to force me out of the village?"

Judging from the gasps, my question startled most villagers. He sneered at me before answering my question.

"Black Thumb Betty's...more like Black Magic Betty's. You need to shut down that witchcraft-adjacent shop. It's so 17th century."

Stan jumped in, shocked to learn of the true plan behind the anonymous notes.

"I didn't have anything to do with that! I just wanted a few mates to share a pint with. They never told me what the notes said."

I was inclined to believe Stan, so I next turned my attention to Chase and Hunter.

"And what about you two? I thought we had made our peace when your father shelved his expansion plans."

Suitably chastised by their public exposure, Chase and Hunter continued looking at their feet. Clive had made his way over from his stand by this point. He reached forward with both hands, lifting his sons' chins so he could look in their faces.

"Boys, why did you do this?"

Chase took the lead in answering. "We heard you and Mum talking about not wanting to lose us to London. We thought if we could open the veggie BBQ Bistro..."

It was Hunter's turn to jump in, "...and Lewis told us he wanted to update the Hare & Harrow to make it 'less sad'..."

"Then COW would become a modern-day mecca that would attract young people."

Hunter was excited as he finished his brother's thoughts. "We could *be* the trendsetters instead of chasing the trends in London!"

By now, Hortense had joined the group that was surrounding the men. "Did you steal the clove from Mrs Pennyworth and plant it in Black Thumb Betty's?"

Lewis, still appearing glib and pompous in his demeanor, chuckled as he replied.

"That was my idea. Frame *her*," he pointed at me as he spat out that last word, "and then she'd be disqualified from Bake Off."

"It *was* a clove conspiracy!" Hortense sputtered.

Moira pushed her way to the middle of the scene, pointing at Lewis, Chase, and Hunter in turn. "Modern-day mecca, my foot. Rowan has done more to drag this village into the twenty-first century than all of you combined."

She then sidled up beside her grandson, pinching his ear between her fingers as she began to drag him away. "You'll not be working in *my* pub ever again. And you can forget any notion of inheriting it now."

She looked over her shoulder as she moved towards the entrance. "I'm sorry, Rowan, for my grandson's part in all this. He'll be heading back to his parents' home immediately."

My head was spinning, and I didn't know where to turn or what to say. I was saved by my father, who suddenly appeared at my side. He wrapped his arm around my shoulder and spoke for both of us.

"My daughter isn't going anywhere. Her home is in this village, thanks to my sister Betty. And I'll be staying nearby to ensure Black Thumb Betty's stays open and drama-free."

My father was moving back to England! I couldn't have been happier at his announcement. I turned towards him and leaned in for the hug I knew was coming. Until I remembered that Cinnamon had talked. In front of the entire village.

Pulling away from my father, I turned to the closest person, Hortense.

"Why isn't anyone surprised about Cinnamon?"

"Hmm? The talking cat? Oh, we've known for some time."

"You knew?! Did Betty know you know?"

"Uncertain. But my suspicion is no. We wanted to help her preserve some of the mystique of Black Thumb Betty's."

I was flabbergasted by Hortense's revelation. That was one secret I wouldn't need to keep anymore. I looked around to find Tilda in the crowd, heartened to see that Arthur had joined her. His arm was firmly place around her shoulders and she was leaning into him. Just behind them, Reverend Primrose looked at me and nodded. And with that, the Catmint Council was disbanded.

"Puppies!" A squeal erupted near the door. Ellie Place had just arrived with her four children, who had proceeded to flop on the ground with Pudding and Pickles. Petunia, sensing an opportunity to cavort with her two favorite groups, sat down beside the youngest Place.

I motioned for Gideon to join me beside the melee of arms and paws. Looking down at the scene, I shared a knowing glance with Petunia. Somehow, she knew what I was plotting and smiled in agreement.

"Gideon, I'd like to introduce you to my sister, Petunia. She loves children and is looking for a job."

I looked up at my father who nodded and jumped in. He knew where I was going with this. "That's right. Now, that I'm moving to the area, I can help Piper with Blooming Brews and Elspeth's care. Petunia, I can tell you are withering away in the tea shop. I know we haven't known each other long, but I hope you'll allow me to take your place there."

The biggest smile broke out on Petunia's face. It looked like she was going to accept my father—our father—in her life after all. Gideon cleared his throat to get her attention.

"If you're interested in a job, Petunia, I would like to hire you as a nanny for my lovely wife, Ellie." He pointed at my father, "If Reg is okay with it, you're welcome to bring Pudding and Pickles along with you anytime."

Petunia looked up at our father expectantly. One sharp little nod was all it took to have the room erupt in squeals and yips of delight. No one could tell which sounds came from dogs and which from humans, adult or child.

27

Sunday
The Day after the Great Harvest Bake Off

As I awoke, a thought kept coming back to me that I couldn't shake. While the senders of one note had been identified, I was still no closer to learning who had sent me the burnt page from *Betty's Steep Secrets*. Sighing as I sat up, I realized my list of mysteries was not complete. But I would shelve it for now, as I wanted to reminisce about everything that had happened at the Bake Off.

This year's Great Harvest Bake Off had ended in a draw, with the judges awarding every participant with at least one award. My cardamom latte won "Best New Beverage", while Aunt Betty's honey-thyme tea received an honorable mention. It had been an exhausting day, full of drama, and I was savoring my first quiet morning in a while. Cinnamon sauntered down from the suite as I took my last sip of coffee.

He had truly been the star of the Bake Off, solving the mystery of the anonymous note and putting to rest the secret of his speaking ability. This morning, he looked pleased as punch with his newfound celebrity.

I placed his bowl of warm milk on the floor for him. Now that he had his collar, there was no need for me to crush cardamom pods or steep cinnamon tea to have a conversation with him. And now that the village was in on the secret, there was no need for the limiter to hide his abilities.

I left him to lap up his milk in silence, plotting how I would broach the topic I was dying to ask him. He jumped up next to me on the couch, turning around three times before settling down to groom himself.

"Cinnamon, I have to ask, you know why Betty named you Cinnamon, don't you?"

He paused mid-lick, his extremely long tongue hanging out of his mouth. "Perhaps."

"Why didn't you tell me?"

"Why didn't you ask me?"

"Touché. And well played."

He went back to licking himself just as Arthur and Rory entered the shop. I hadn't bothered to lock the door the night before. It was a village, after all, and I finally felt safe and at home in it.

"Good morning to both of you! To what do I owe this pleasure?"

Arthur chuckled nervously as he leaned on his cane. I coaxed Cinnamon off the couch and motioned for them to join me. Rory chose the seat next to me, ceding the more accessible armchair for his elderly uncle-cousin. He waited patiently for Arthur to begin speaking.

"Rory and I had a long conversation on our drive to

London. It seems you've been harboring secrets for both of us."

I leaned back on the couch and raised my arms in the air. No more secrets! I couldn't have been happier.

"So, you both know?"

"When Arthur told me his meeting was about announcing his retirement from Nettle & Nudge, I came clean about my mum's request that I return to the farm."

"Does that mean you'll both be in the village full time?"

Rory looked at me expectantly, encouraged by the enthusiasm he heard in my voice. His immediate acceptance of Cinnamon's speaking ability had started to sway my feelings for him.

"It does. Does that mean you may be open to a date?"

I smiled at him, realizing I was ready to explore more than friendship with this kind, caring, and handsome man.

"It does."

He smiled back, but our brief moment was interrupted by a flurry of activity outside the shop. Looking over my shoulder, I saw a whole host of people and animals, jockeying to enter Black Thumb Betty's. Laughing at the mêlée, I stood up to open the door for the crowd.

In tromped all three Smeaton men, Piper, Tilda, my father, and the pugs. Pudding and Pickles took center stage, as they ran to Cinnamon, bowing at his feet. We giggled at their unwavering dedication to the feline and I'm sure Cinnamon was loving every minute of it. Piper took the opportunity to speak up.

"I've just come from Whiskerleigh, and I have loads of exciting news!"

She pointed at the Smeatons before continuing. "Let's start with you. Chase, Hunter, there's a 'for sale' sign on The Wagging Spoon, at the corner of Tabby Row and Biscuit

Street. It would be a great location for your veggie BBQ Bistro."

The young men clapped their hands together and jumped up and down with glee. They looked like a couple of twelve-year-olds as they turned to their father, hope in their eyes.

"Can we go see the property? Please, please, please?"

Clive Smeaton chuckled at his adult sons' exuberance. "Well, perhaps your mother's wish is coming true. She wanted you 'close by, but not underfoot.' Thank you, Piper, for the information. We'll go look into it straightaway."

As they exited the shop, Piper then turned to our father —it still felt odd for me to think of him as someone else's father, but I was quickly getting used to it. In truth, I liked the sound of it.

"Reg, I mean Dad. I mean, is it okay if I call you Dad?"

She grasped at her hands nervously, gulping in air as she scanned the room. My father reached out and patted her shoulder, a beaming smile lighting up his entire face. His voice caught as he responded.

"Nothing would make me happier, dear."

Relieved, Piper continued. "When I was in Dr. Sniffle's Pet Surgery—I'll get back to that in a moment," she interjected when she saw my look of confusion. We had agreed to forego the limiter for Cinnamon, since the village was in on the secret. I was bursting to know why she still visited the surgery, but my curiosity would have to wait until Piper finished sharing all her exciting news. "Anyhoo, Dr. Sniffle told me that his suite upstairs is available. And the best part? Pets are not only welcome, they're encouraged!"

"Dad, this is great! Whiskerleigh is only twelve miles away. We'll practically be neighbors."

My father snorted a laugh at my 'neighbors' comment,

as he recalled my reticence to let he and my mother stay in Brooklyn when I was still living in New York. Piper and I shared an amused glance at his snort. She shook her head and grinned, likely remembering my comment that this particular behavior was one that made me first suspect the connection between them.

"If you're alright with that, Rowan. And you and Petunia, of course."

Piper walked closer to him, opening her hands as she spoke. "Well, since you've already offered to help with Mum and the shop, it makes sense for you to find somewhere to live that's not too far away."

My father nodded as the idea of living so close to his three daughters took shape in his mind. I could almost see the wheels turning in his brain.

"Quite right. I'll do it! How do I get in touch with this Dr. Sniffle?"

Piper pulled a piece of paper out of her pocket and handed it to our father. "Here's the number for the surgery. He's expecting your call."

My father dashed behind the counter and picked up the phone. I turned my attention back to Piper.

"So, why were you in the surgery in the first place?"

She smiled and pulled something—two somethings, to be precise—out of her other pocket.

"Collars! For Pudding and Pickles, so they can talk too."

I smacked my hand against my forehead. "Of course! No need to keep it a secret anymore. Let's go get them prepped for the pooches."

We raced towards the kitchen to prep the necessary formulation that would give the pugs the power of speech too. When we returned to the shop, Tilda and Arthur were snuggled up on the couch, with all three animals resting at their feet. My father and Rory were noticeably absent, as Rory had offered to drive him to Whiskerleigh. Since Arthur would no longer need the car or Rory for his regular jaunts into London, he had agreed to let Rory use it as a part-time shuttle between the two villages.

Another chime of the bell and I turned to see Peter Bramble entering the shop. He appeared well-rested and well-groomed, much different than our initial encounter.

"Peter! It's so great to see you again." After introducing him to everyone assembled, I yielded the floor to him.

"Thank you, Rowan. I can't thank you enough for helping me in my time of need."

I waved my hand in thanks. "It's what anyone in our village would have done. Are you heading home now?"

"I am, but I wanted to tell you that I'll be recommending Cresswell-on-Wyrd as a 'must see' destination in the National Rambling Association guidebook."

Tilda squealed her delight. "That will definitely help us become a 'modern-day mecca', as the young people so desire."

Peter chuckled awkwardly. "Not sure about 'modern-day', but it will definitely boost visitors. Most of the members of the NRA are north of 50 years of age. But they have money to burn."

Arthur chimed in. "Well then, we shall welcome them with open arms. Perhaps I should look at converting the outbuilding on my estate into overnight accommodation."

He was clearly plotting his post-retirement. As Peter nodded and headed towards the door, Arthur and Tilda took the opportunity to head back to his country home. They were engaged in an animated discussion about whether Tilda should move her belongings out of the guest suite and into the master bedroom. Love was definitely in the air in Cresswell-on-Wyrd

Piper and I looked at each other and nodded in agreement. It was time to unleash the hounds. As I reached down to replace the collar around Pudding's neck with the improved, speaking version, Piper repeated the same process with Pickles.

Satisfied with the collars, Piper and I stepped back to observe the pugs. The dogs stood up and sniffed each other's necks before opening their mouths to speak. It was a cacophony of sound, as they tried to be heard above each other.

"What's that, sis?"

"I can't hear you, bro."

"Speak up! My voice is drowning out yours."

"What?"

With one swift movement, Cinnamon gently swatted both pugs. The effect was immediate, and they turned and followed Cinnamon to the recently vacated couch. In the sunlit shop window, Pudding and Pickles curled up on either side of Cinnamon. The cat muttered to himself as he closed his eyes.

"If this isn't the start of another adventure, I'll eat my collar—preferably with a side of cream."

The pugs barked back—in French.

Piper and I grinned at each other. I held my finger up to my lips and motioned for her to help me carry the sandwich board onto the street. I had updated the sign last night before turning in:

Black Thumb Betty's:
Curiously Comforting Since 1973

On the other side was the shop's new, secondary slogan:

The Cat's Cup:
Brews That Speak for Themselves

The End

Scan the QR code to follow those pesky pugs into a new adventure!

This is a work of fiction. Names, characters, places, and incidents are either the product of the author's imagination or are used fictitiously, and any resemblance to actual persons, living or dead, business establishments, events, or locales is entirely coincidental.

Sterczyk, Amanda, author

Cinnamon and the Clove Conspiracy / Amanda Sterczyk.

Issued in electronic format & paperback versions.

ISBN: 978-1-0697175-5-9

Editors: Margaret Gobie, Rebekka Lee

Cover Design: Melody Simmons

ABOUT THE AUTHOR

Amanda Sterczyk is a Canadian author whose brain recently pivoted from push-ups to plot twists. Best known until now as a seniors' fitness expert and founder of The Move More Institute™, Amanda has been featured on CBC Radio, CTV Morning Live, Thrive Global, and other outlets that suggest she knows what she's talking about. Her wellness motto was, "Move more, feel better." These days, it's more like, "Sip tea, pet cat, solve fictional crimes."

Amanda lives in Ottawa, Canada with her husband, two adult children (who still live at home and haven't been written into any mysteries... yet), and one very clingy cat who insists she did not help write the books—just napped dramatically on the manuscripts.

www.ingramcontent.com/pod-product-compliance
Lightning Source LLC
LaVergne TN
LVHW090945080826
845145LV00003B/900

* 9 7 8 1 0 6 9 7 1 7 5 5 9 *